DEPARTMENT A-13 AERO-MARSHAL
★ UNITED STATES OF AMERICA ★

A·13

CUSTODIENS CAELA

JIM BEARD

DUANE SPURLOCK

This special edition is limited to 150 copies signed by the authors.

AIRSHIP HUNTERS

AIRSHIP HUNTERS

JIM BEARD & DUANE SPURLOCK

METEOR HOUSE

AIRSHIP HUNTERS

by Jim Beard & Duane Spurlock

Meteor House

ISBN 978-0-9905673-0-1

First Signed Edition Limited to 150 Copies

TABLE OF CONTENTS

Dedicated to The Little Woman, the enticing Mystery
I hope never to completely solve. —Jim Beard

With love to my sons, who—since the bedtimes I read
Treasure Island and *Kidnapped*—have a great enjoyment
for mystery and adventure. —Duane Spurlock

ACKNOWLEDGMENTS

Meteor House and the authors would like to thank the following readers who preordered this limited edition novel and helped it take flight:

Stephanie Wagner, Anthony R. Cardno, Art Sippo, Michael R. Brown, Josh Reynolds, Steven Smith, Georgina Eloise Spiteri, Madeleine Lucy Spiteri, Claire Spiteri, Shawn Vogt, Paul Niedernhofer, Thomas Potter, Anthony Kapolka, Scott Gibson, Katherine Stites, Derek Cockerham, Elizabeth Cseri, Laurie Wolberton, Katherine Shaw, David Rains, Chuck Welch, Kim & Scott Turk, Max Mathis, Mark Martinez, Theodore Gregory, Ralph Grasso, Lucas Garrett, Robert Deis, Cathy Keibler, Alexander Grant, Mike Hunter, Scott Selle, Terry Krieger, Eric Timm, Blue Derkin, J. Scott Radel, Bertha Hunt, Bill Kirschbaum, Logan County Public Library, Dan Silvers, Ben Schellhase, Elizabeth Silvers, Ronald Weston, Russell Wright, Charles Millhouse, Larry "Chile Pepper" Brown, John Del Col, Julie Moore, Lige B. Rushing III, Lisa Eckert, Patricia Wildman, James Caliban, M.D., John Bruening, Mike Chomko, Herbert Jacobi, PulpFest, Don Youel, Edward Stuart, Lynn Carter, Raymond Navor, Kathleen Honigford, Aries Ropp, Joanie Asendorf, Donna Legree Rohlff, Jennifer Collins, Rick Lai, Harold Pickard, Enrico Barisione, Terry Chio, Steven Hager, Ken Kessler, Rodney Rhodus, the JoeErin Mathias Family, Trent Spurlock, Elie Harriet, Martha Spurlock, Robert Craig, and Ralph Carlson.

Additionally, Jim Beard would like to thank Duane Spurlock, who believed in him and the concept and helped flesh it out into something far beyond its humble initial thoughts. Duane Spurlock would like to thank Jim Beard, for trusting in him enough to share the world of the Aero-Marshals. Together they would both like to thank M. S. Corley for his wonderful skills in translating their prose descriptions into a delightful cover illustration, and the entire Meteor House crew: Christopher Paul Carey, Michael Croteau, Win Scott Eckert, Keith Howell, Ray Riethmeier, and Paul Spiteri, who made everything better.

ORCHESTRATIONS
Jim Beard

June 1897

A irships, sir?"

Major Wellington gave the officer who sat in front of his desk a pointed look, one that spoke of some slight annoyance at the question.

"Yes. Coined by a newspaper writer. Seems to have stuck."

Lieutenant Michael Valiantine looked down at the dress hat he held in his hands and back up at the major. He said nothing, unsure of what he could say about it all.

"This," Wellington said, tapping a file that lay on his desk, "says you've been prone to speak your mind at times. Well, speak it, man."

Valiantine had been away from the service almost a full year and everything around him seemed odd. Nothing looked familiar, though he couldn't see how that much could have changed in a relatively short span of time to afford him such disquiet. The major in particular came off as a different sort of man, though he hadn't been Valiantine's direct superior before the lieutenant had been wounded and ordered to convalesce for an "indeterminate period" after his release from the Army hospital. Wellington's office looked rearranged, a status that nudged the lieutenant into the uncomfortable position of desiring nothing more than to march around and set it back to right.

Instead, Valiantine reached up and opened another file the major had set at the edge of his desk for him to peruse. Inside it lay several sheets of paper, all of them choked with reports of "airships."

"I'll go over it again, Valiantine. They tell me you're fit for duty, so I expect you to listen and get a firm handle on the situation."

Wellington leaned forward in his chair, took a cheroot from a wooden box, and lit it from an ornate lighter he was using as a paperweight. Valiantine hadn't known the man to smoke before.

"First sighted in California last year," the major said around puffs on the stick. "Several reports in the local papers. Big things, some of them moving at a rapid pace, others just floating there, in mid-air."

The man paused. Valiantine wondered if his own reactions were being gauged by Wellington. He felt suddenly very self-conscious of his new moustache and his over regulation-length hair, both grown during his off-time.

"Unlike anything anybody'd ever seen before," the major continued. "And able to move at a speed that staggered the imagination. And no two of these things described alike in their physical make-up.

"Then, they started moving eastward."

Valiantine turned one report over to glance at the next. He spied the word "Nebraska" there.

"Seem to be following rail lines," the major said, puffing away. "Or at least that's what some genius somewhere deduced. Can't nod to the validity of that. Anyway, these airships started appearing over Wyoming, Nebraska . . . Illinois. Latest reports were only just last month, right up to the Illinois-Indiana line. Then, nothing."

The lieutenant looked up at Wellington. "Flocks of birds? Eagles?"

"No, absolutely not."

"Cloud formations?"

"At night? Look at the damn reports, Valiantine."

"Then, if there's anything to this, someone's made some advances, certainly."

The major appraised him with half-open eyes. "Yes. But who? And how?"

Valiantine's head swam. He hadn't expected to return to anything like this. In the service since he was eighteen, he'd been on "detached special duty" for almost ten years, operating out of the War Department building in Washington, D.C. and going where he was needed, doing what he was ordered to do. During his convalescence at Virginia Beach, on the ocean, something substantial had occurred. He'd met a woman and began to question thoughts of returning to active duty.

The woman. No, that was unfair. She was Eileen, but Valiantine had joked with her that no name could ever do her pretty features justice. She in turn quoted Shakespeare, telling him there was "no thought of pleasing him when she was christened." From that moment on he was decidedly smitten with the woman, yet their flirtation did not exactly extend to love though, and thoughts of his career began to weigh heavily upon him. Finally, he had made his decision.

Eileen had failed to comprehend his instinctual desire to return to the service; truth be told, he didn't fully understand it himself. Despite the rare happiness he'd experienced with her, something pulled him back, an intangible compulsion that ultimately drove a wedge between him and a woman with whom he thought he might be able to spend the rest of his life. Instead, he returned, unsure of what exactly he thought he was doing and why.

Valiantine had been wounded when a cannon had exploded near him on a test range in New York, pitting one whole side of him with shrapnel. The doctors said he'd been lucky not to have taken any to the head, but deep inside he felt as if he had. His once-clear thoughts were no longer as sharp as before his accident; though his body had healed, the lieutenant doubted he was entirely rested. He often awoke to the sound of the exploding cannon ringing in his brain.

On his first day back on duty, he was called in to Major Wellington's office, a man he never much liked, and told what on the surface seemed to be a fairy story.

"Lilenthal made a glider six years ago," the major grumbled. "Maxim got close a few years later, and then that disaster in Massachusetts last year. But the latest leap was a 'bi-plane' experiment in Indiana, also just last year. Went south, as was expected."

"Indiana? And you say these airships were last seen approaching Indiana? Could there be something to that?"

Wellington speared the lieutenant with a look. "That's what we want *you* to find out."

"Sir," Valiantine replied, "why not just send a few troops in to check things over?"

"Done that," the major said, stabbing out his barely smoked cigar in a glass ashtray with a spark of annoyance. It was all the lieutenant could do not to wipe away some of the ash that had fallen outside the dish. Valiantine wanted to bite his own hand to still it from reaching out.

"Caused too much of a stir," Wellington continued, "and so we realized we couldn't operate out in the open and hope to learn anything useful. That's where you come in, Valiantine. You're going in, but in mufti."

It was almost as if a series of steel gratings had popped up around the lieutenant, feeling trapped as he did just then. It made his insides squirm.

"With all due respect, sir, I don't feel I'm the right man for this."

"And yet," Wellington said with clear annoyance, stabbing one finger down upon the officer's file again, "*this* says your experience with covert work is rather extensive. Ireland in '86, Samoa in '88, South Dakota in '90, Wyoming in '92, and then of course, Nicaragua last year, before you were wounded. Should I go on, Lieutenant?"

Valiantine said nothing. The backward feeling of the office and of the man in front of him grew so strong as to cause him physical pain in his temples. This had often been the case when he'd been confronted with discordant stimuli, and the odd mix of the familiar and unfamiliar of the major and his office certainly qualified as that.

"No, I don't need to go on because you are the man for the job. And this is a direct order."

The lieutenant gazed out the window, at the executive mansion beyond and the trees blossoming around it. He sighed, yet very quietly.

"Sir, is the . . . supposition that this is the work of a foreign power, or that it is domestic?" he inquired, facing the major once more.

Wellington nodded, seemingly pleased. "Good. Good. You're thinking again. Both of those are somewhat frightening questions, eh? Some other country flying things above our heads without our knowledge or say-so . . . or our own citizens doing the same?

"That's for you to uncover, Lieutenant. And this goes all the way to the top office, by the way. The President's looked at that file, read it, so there's some weight being placed upon it."

"Where should I begin?"

"Indiana. We don't care where. Your choice."

"And what should I do there?"

"Look into it, Valiantine. Keep watch. And report back. Dismissed."

As Valiantine rode the chugging Chesapeake & Ohio into Indiana, clouds outside the window turned to great sailing vessels in the sky.

The train ride had afforded him some peace of mind, and he found his thoughts clearing to line up and be assessed. He felt it was now possible he might regain something of his old self and carry out his orders, no matter how vague or fanciful they might seem to him.

In planning his attack on the problem of where to begin his "watch," Valiantine turned to a map of the state of Indiana and narrowed his focus. He immediately dismissed Chanute and Paul's Dune Park flight experiment the previous year in Indiana as too incongruous with the known airship sightings and swung his attention to what he imagined as a kind of trajectory of the impossible vehicles—if even vehicles they were.

Ultimately, the rail line he rode would end in Chicago, but he'd no intention of riding it to that conclusion. If his research held any weight at all, the latest glimpse of a supposed airship occurred miles to the south of the big city, somewhere below Gary, Indiana. Valiantine intended to disembark in either Peru or potentially the next stop and then make his way northwest, watching and observing all the way.

As a plan went, it lacked clearly defined parameters. This niggled away at the lieutenant's usually well-ordered approach to a mission, but he had far less to go on than possibly ever before in his career.

In short, he would be not much more precise than a blind man stumbling around in the dark.

In a way, he understood and somewhat sympathized with his superiors at the War Department and their concerns. A bloody conflict with Spain loomed on the horizon, a foregone conclusion to a bout of saber-rattling and bellyaching the likes of which had not been seen for many years in the halls of government. But, that said, the thought that the Spaniards had somehow crafted and launched a fleet of flying machines over America came across as overly ludicrous. War would most certainly come, and soon, but the lieutenant felt secure in his opinion it would not be waged in the skies above them.

He waved down a boy on the platform at Marion from his window and bought a newspaper. Flipping through it, Valiantine hoped to gain a sense of Indiana's cultural mindset. Within its pages he found reports of farming and mining, political squabbles, and the like. The most interesting bit of news sprung from an article detailing a series of robberies throughout the central portion of the state, the latest one in a bank in Lafayette.

The swaying of the train and the progression of type across the page lulled the lieutenant into dozing in his seat. The flat countryside moved past him out the window, the sailing vessels of the clouds forgotten as he nodded off into a light sleep.

The sharp, shattering blast of a whistle brought him back to consciousness with a start and he realized with cold dread that he'd missed his stop in Peru. Valiantine gazed out of his window and tried to make out the station's sign through the thick smoke that choked the platform.

Finally, he made it out: Manitou.

The name was unfamiliar to him; he didn't remember it from his perusal of his maps. The whistle blew again, signaling the train's imminent departure and, in a burst of reckless adrenalin, Valiantine leapt from his seat, snatched his bag from the upper rack, and swung out the door and onto the platform.

A split second later, the train lurched and pulled away from the platform. A uniformed railwayman stood with hands on hips nearby, glaring at the lieutenant and shaking his head from side to side in disbelief. Valiantine tipped his hat to the man and made his way into the station, pulling his watch from his vest as he entered.

Stepping up to a large map that hung on the station's wall, he studied it in hopes of pinpointing his location. He found himself landed almost fifteen miles outside of Peru, and a small trek south of a lake also named Manitou.

The lieutenant grinned a bit at his impulsive behavior, picked up his bag and went in search of a hotel.

Manitou, Indiana would have to do for a start, he reasoned.

A few hours later, after checking into the small town's single hotel, he found himself, of all things, attending a town meeting.

Valiantine looked down at his civilian attire and fussed with it a bit, wondering for the hundredth time since he left his room over the extent of his ability to blend in with the locals. He'd chosen a plain brown suit with no ornamentation save for a straw hat and his watch and chain. He'd even eschewed spats for a solid pair of commonplace boots.

As entertainment went, a town meeting wasn't exactly high on the bill for a pleasurable experience, but Valiantine knew that immersing himself in the heart of a populace, in a venue designed to air thoughts and debate, would potentially reward him far more than a saloon would.

At first glance, Manitou appeared to be a typical small town in the heartland of the country. Valiantine hadn't yet gotten a lock on the industry that fed the town, but, he told himself, he was more concerned with what hung above it than what transpired at ground level. And if the first several minutes of the meeting were any indication, Manitou, with its population of slightly more than a thousand citizens, had a monopoly on mundanity.

There came a loud noise from off to one side of the meeting hall. Forty sets of eyes narrowed and focused on the disturbance. Valiantine rose a bit from his seat in the back of the room to glimpse the source of the commotion.

A man at a side door jostled another man, clearly trying to block him from entering. The second man had become quite vocal and was yelling his protestation over his treatment by the first man.

"Can' keep me out, you corn-fed idiot! I got rights, too! I went t'school here! I got papers! Papers!"

Valiantine saw that people around him were beginning to wag their heads and even snicker at the man's antics. Low whispering spread throughout the small crowd.

The man was dressed in what could charitably be called a haphazard fashion. He wore a pair of pants perhaps one size too big for him, with only suspenders holding them on to his lanky frame. He wore no socks, only a pair of worn shoes, and no vest underneath his well-patched topcoat. A small, dusty bowler sat perched on the man's head, barely containing a wild mop of salt-and-pepper hair.

"Take him out, take him out," said the man at the front of the room who led the meeting. "We've no time for such foolishness."

More men appeared, ringing themselves around the odd character. Valiantine thought immediately they seemed much too big and burly and in excessive number to eject one, down-on-his luck townsperson.

One of the men clamped a hand around the mouth of the odd man and together all five of the supposed guardians dragged him through the door and outside. The door slammed shut behind them, echoing loudly in its finality.

Overly curious, the lieutenant rose from his bench and slipped away from the meeting to follow after the entourage.

He exited through a door on the opposite wall and made his way around the building to the other side. There he found an alleyway, dark and disused, yet now occupied by the odd man and his ejectors. The men had their charge up against a brick wall, wagging fingers in his face. Valiantine listened in.

"We've told you before to keep your damn mouth shut, Mr. Perklee," one of the men said. "This town's sick of you, hear? You and your crazy talk will be the death of you."

The odd man squeezed his eyes shut and popped them open once again. "Boys, boys! Let me talk! Let me talk! It relieves the pressure—"

A fist shot out from the throng of men around him, planting itself in Perklee's belly. He doubled over, moaning.

The lieutenant frowned, watching the scene from his vantage point. It was of no concern of his. A local matter, a dispute he had no business even witnessing. It had nothing to do with him.

He turned away with the sounds of more delivered punches and the yelps of the odd man washing over him.

"Oh, my!" Perklee shouted. "Oh my Lord! They can't find me like this! They won't like it! They won't like it! The voices will be very angry!"

Valiantine came to an abrupt stop. He turned back to the melee, listening intently.

"The voices of the skies!" the odd man said. "The skies! The skies!"

The attackers grew tired of the beating quickly, and Valiantine waited for them to depart before moving in to sweep up the odd man from the alleyway and offering to remove him to his home. The man nodded silently, blood trickling from his nose and the corner of his mouth, and pointed the way.

Their conjoined journey proved to be a long walk to the north, beyond the confines of the town, and ended at the southernmost portion of Lake Manitou at a small cabin that sat on its serene shore.

Valiantine felt a chill in the air, the last dregs of winter's hold on the flat Indiana landscape. His charge had said precious little on their shuffling march to the cabin, granting an awkward air to the situation as he half-carried Perklee along. The lieutenant hoped what he'd heard from the man's own mouth in the alley were not simply the ravings of the inebriated, but something tangible for him to bolster his mission.

It seemed a very weak hope by the time they'd reached the cabin.

Perklee's home was a cluttered mess; Valiantine's often-prickly sense of order roiled at the sight of it. There was no actual filth present, but the man's housekeeping left much to be desired. His belongings sat everywhere, with no real rhyme or reason to be discerned by an outsider, though the lieutenant assumed the man himself could divine an order to the disarray.

Setting his charge down carefully in a threadbare chair, he looked around the cabin's main room, settling his attention on the many framed documents that hung on the walls. Valiantine discovered with mild surprise the man was an educated individual, with diplomas and other various forms of official documentation to prove it. Glancing back at the wreck of human life that sat nearly insensate in the chair, he found it difficult to reconcile it all.

"Mr. Perklee," he said, kneeling down next to the chair, his voice quiet at first, but then increasing in volume. "I'd like to ask you some questions, sir."

The odd man stirred, eyes attempting to focus on Valiantine. One hand lifted and pointed at a shelf off to one side. A bottle sat there.

With some disgust, the lieutenant fetched the bottle and handed it to the man, who pulled out its cork and drank sloppily from it.

"Why did those men beat you, back in the town?" the lieutenant asked, witnessing animation creeping back into Perklee.

"Didn' wan' me t'talk," came the whispery, slurred reply.

"Why? Talk about what?"

"Not import'nt."

"It is to me, sir. What can you tell me about it? About the skies?"

Perklee's eyes widened. "Oh, *that*. There's a story there . . ."

"Tell me, please," Valiantine said, expectant.

The man shifted in the chair, turning himself slightly to face the lieutenant.

"'Twas music. I heard music. In the sky."

Valiantine silently urged the man to continue.

"The branches, of the trees, you know. Kept breakin'. So I said I better see what was doin' it. Then I heard th'music. Like an orchestra. Yeah . . . jus' like 'n orchestra, but up above."

He pointed heavenward, as if to press home the distinction.

"Heard 'Far 'bove Cayuga's Waters' firs,' then . . . then . . . wha' was it? 'Beautiful Dreamer,' 'm guessin'. Than it really kicked off, wit' Schubert. Whole orchestra. Was nice, real nice. Th'strings was, was partic'larly good, you know?"

He paused. Once again, Valiantine reflected upon Perklee's degeneration from learned man to slurring derelict.

"Do you like music, young gen'lman?"

The lieutenant found himself unable to answer at first, but soon nodded and mumbled in the affirmative.

"What then, sir?"

"Well!" the man said with relish. "Then I heard th'voices—a lot of voices. Maybe was clappin' firs'? Anyway, th'voices sounded like . . . like a gay party, you know? Like a gay, grand party up in the air."

Perklee began to drift away with his memories. Valiantine reached out and shook him a bit, by the arms. A stack of books that sat nearby fell over, tumbling and sliding onto the already-cluttered floor. He resisted the urge to pick them up and set them back the way they were.

"Did—did you talk to them?" he asked. "To the voices?"

He heard himself saying the words, but found it difficult to credit them. Was this really what he'd come all the way to Indiana to do? Question a possible mental patient?

"Yeah." Perklee nodded, his eyes refocusing. "I yelled up at them! 'Wha's th'meanin' of all this?' I said. Ver' loud. Ver' loud. 'Wha' may I ask 's goin' on up there, m'good people?'"

"And they . . . they replied, did they?"

"No' a' firs, m'fellow. No a' firs' . . . but after a mom'nt or two . . . they t'rew some *food* down t'me."

Valiantine blinked, wholly confounded. "Food?"

"Yeah," the man said, "an' I still got some."

The lieutenant immediately demanded to see whatever it was Perklee called "food." The man acquiesced, but only after a promise that Valiantine would not remove it from the cabin.

He brought out a small covered plate from the cabin's tiny pantry and with a clumsy flourish whisked the cover away. On the plate sat a lump—vaguely cube-shaped—of a pale, porous-looking substance. Valiantine stared at it, then asked if he could observe it under better light.

In the glow of an oil lamp, he saw it resembled bread in a way, yet with no discernable crust or darkened edges. No smell came from it, but it looked reasonably edible, even appetizing. The niggling compulsion to pick it up and bring it to his tongue and lips was strong, but he saw how Perklee watched him and he tamped down on it.

"Where?" he croaked at the man, his mouth gone dry. "Where did this all occur, Mr. Perklee?"

The odd man peered at him queerly in the light of the lamp. "Who are you, sir? Have we been intr'duced?"

Many different scenarios flashed through the lieutenant's mind, many things he could tell the man, but he chose the truth.

"I am with the United States Army, sir. My name is Valiantine."

"Oh!" Perklee said, "I heard there wa' soldiers in th' area!"

Then he crumpled in a heap on the floor.

"Where?" he asked the odd man again as he tried to pick him up. "Where did it all happen? It's very important that you tell me, sir!"

In a hushed tone, Perklee described an area only a mile from the cabin, along the shore of the lake and at the foot of some low hills, which were rare in the region. The lieutenant spied a bed in another room of the cabin and he left the man there, nearly unconscious. Making his way out into the woods he picked up a trail he reasoned would lead him to the spot in question.

It matched Perklee's description well. Once there, Valiantine stood and listened to the night.

It took only a handful of minutes before an overwhelming sense of the ridiculous crept into his mind and took root.

Staring out onto the stillness of Lake Manitou, he saw it all as a fool's errand, perhaps even some sort of hazing by his superiors for his lengthy convalescence. No matter; he'd see it through to the end, no matter how devoid of prospects.

He thought back over the contents of the file he'd been shown. Many of the reports of airships came from newspapers, and their reporters were surely not above making up stories to sell more copies. How many airship sightings were fabricated? Most of them, he reasoned. All of them, perhaps.

Still . . . he thought of Perklee. Why had he received the treatment he had at the hands of the men in town? That at least was a fact; they beat him soundly and with malice. How did it figure into his mission?

Valiantine shook his head ruefully. It didn't, obviously. He'd stumbled into something in Manitou that was none of his business and made connections that had no basis in reality. He'd rectify the situation by steering clear of it and moving north, as he'd originally planned.

Then, a flash of insight sent a sharp, stabbing pain through his brain: he had to get back to the cabin, and quickly.

The lieutenant covered the distance swiftly and arrived at the odd man's home in short order. Everything looked the same as when he'd left. Opening the door to the abode, he called out to Perklee.

Receiving no reply, Valiantine ran to the bed where he had left the odd man and discovered him to be gone.

Worry and doubt assailed the lieutenant. He turned to go and found himself facing several figures, standing there in the darkness, glaring at him.

The first of the men came at the lieutenant with a roundhouse punch, which he managed to block, but not the second and third such blows. Staggered from the unexpected onslaught, he hopped backward and raised his fists, steeling himself for what was to come next.

One of the other men jumped into the fray, aiming a blow at Valiantine's midsection. The lieutenant took some of the force out of it by deflecting it off his forearm, but a swift uppercut sent him reeling. With a grunt of exertion, a third man slugged him in the side of the head and what sounded to Valiantine like a chuckle of mirth. He saw stars and heard roaring in his ears, his face reddening over his inability to properly defend himself. Another blow caught him on the collarbone, and yet another on his chin.

Valiantine dropped to one knee, his head whirling, and he knew it was all over for him. The men surrounded him en masse, their fists and feet providing a cacophony of pain. This went on for an undetermined length of time, the impact of the violence playing havoc with his sense of it.

Valiantine's pistol lay in his valise in his hotel room, back in

Manitou. He'd fallen out of the habit of carrying it, and as he rolled with the punches from his attackers, he regretted its absence. In the future, he'd remedy the oversight.

Blessedly, he remembered enough from his past experiences and folded himself up into a ball to take the worst of it in less vulnerable places on his body, though those spots still often ached from his injuries the year before. As he slipped into unconsciousness, the lieutenant hoped he'd be able to walk away from the beating a more-or-less whole man.

The men said nothing during the assault; no warnings or reasons came forth. They left him there in Perklee's cabin, seemingly caring little if he were alive or dead.

He awoke in a mental fog the next morning. Valiantine uncurled himself to a symphony of aches and pains, but very much still alive.

The cabin's owner, he found, was still missing, and, he also discovered after a rudimentary search of the place, so too was the "food" from the supposed airship. He wondered if the man himself had taken it or perhaps his kidnappers, if Perklee had been waylaid and taken away by force at all. If he had sobered up, he may have left on his own, taking his precious substance from the sky with him.

Setting a fallen chair upright, Valiantine sat down on it gingerly and fought back a desire to straighten the cabin. This angered him and he chided himself for the foolish drive for order; what he needed to do was to order his own thoughts and decide if Manitou had served out any scant usefulness to him and his mission.

He heard a branch snap somewhere outside and peered out the window to see a human figure standing at the edge of the line of trees, watching the cabin. The lieutenant stood up quickly, his head swimming, and yelled at the figure.

The man turned tail and moved away swiftly, back into the trees, just as Valiantine assumed he might.

Valiantine swore and ran out of the cabin and toward the spot where the figure had disappeared. Remembering the path he'd taken to where Perklee had encountered the ships, he sped off and down it, glancing sideways into the trees, looking for the opportunity to cut the man off somewhere.

Built for sprinting, the wiry lieutenant forged ahead, despite his past injuries and the recent beating. Hearing someone crashing through the underbrush in the woods and slightly behind him, he abruptly veered off at a ninety-degree angle and propelled himself into the woods on what looked like an old path.

Only seconds later he came to a dead stop in front of the fleeing man, his arms and hands up, ready to stop him or fight him, whatever was necessary.

"Lord!" the man spat, grinding to a halt and almost pitching headlong into the brush. His hand disappeared into the greatcoat he wore, but Valiantine saw the movement and kicked out with his booted foot. He caught the man's wrist with the blow, heard a yelp of pain, and saw a pistol tumble out of the coat and onto the ground.

They stood staring at each other, both of them silent and aware of the pistol lying somewhere between them.

"Law?" the man asked, an average-sized specimen with sandy-colored hair, a short beard, and a forehead littered with small scars. Valiantine remained silent.

The man nodded, his eyes scanning the lieutenant's face and clothing. "Then . . . Army. Yeah, I'd say Army."

Valiantine gave him a curt nod in answer. The man's eyes crinkled at the corners as he smiled slightly and shook his head.

"Daddy fought in the War of the Rebellion. I was too young, just a child, but I wanted to. I see something of him in your bearing."

"My father also fought. We have that in common," Valiantine said, easing back a bit from his position. He swung his chin to one side, back the way from which they had come. "And maybe that cabin."

The man's eyebrows rose. "Okay, maybe so. Tell you what;

you go ahead and pick up that pistol and then maybe we can have a talk. You look like an intelligent fellow. Maybe we have even more in common."

As it turned out, they did. The man introduced himself as Awanai. "Just that, nothing more," he said, and the lieutenant saw the strain of Oriental in him. Together they walked through the woods and to a mostly hidden lean-to among the low hills, not far at all from the spot Valiantine had stood the night before, watching and waiting.

"You live here?" he asked Awanai, walking around the crude structure. "Do the people in . . . ah, of course they do.

"You're the regional bandit, the one they talk about in the newspapers."

The man bowed. "Guilty as charged. Going to turn me in, sir?"

"No," Valiantine said, "I don't give a damn what you're doing, as long as you're not killing people. The papers say you aren't."

Awanai smiled. "Again correct. I've even given the people of Manitou a portion of my, well, ill-gotten gains. It *is* my home-town, after all."

It began to make sense to the lieutenant. The townspeople not only knew Awanai lived outside Manitou, they were most likely ensuring no one else would know. Thus, the beatings and the intimidation of people like Perklee.

The bandit crawled into his lean-to and came back with a bottle. Producing two glasses from a box, he poured out two fingers of the bottle's clear liquid in each and handed one to his guest.

Inwardly, Valiantine flinched at the sight of the dirty glass. The bandit must have seen the slight tic in his face, for he chuckled and pressed the glass into the lieutenant's hand.

"The liquor kills the germs. Drink up."

The moonshine burned an unholy rivulet down his throat but he was determined not to cough as he swallowed. Then, after a good draught of it, he looked back at Awanai.

"How do you know Mr. Perklee?"

The bandit motioned for them to sit down on two tree stumps nearby. Once seated, he swirled his liquor around in his glass and smiled.

"Known him for years," he explained. "He was a professor of mine, back at Notre Dame. A good man. I learned a lot from him. He's nothing now like he was before."

An expression of either disgust or pity or a mingling of both came over the bandit as he spoke.

"But he's still my friend. Folks in town don't like him being out here, talking with me. They're afraid he's going to spill the beans to someone when he's in one of his stupors. I like his company, but I've asked him to stop coming to visit me out here, for his own safety. He's not the only folk I entertain."

"Why does he then?" Valiantine asked, perplexed.

Awanai looked off, toward the lake, then shrugged. "Not entirely sure, friend. He can be a mighty strange old coot when he wants to be. But that shouldn't earn him a beating. I don't condone that."

The lieutenant digested that, unsure of what he could say to the bandit, or what he wanted to say. The situation grew more bizarre with each passing hour and he needed to simplify things before they became so complicated that he found himself on an even more unsure footing.

The bandit poured Valiantine another measure of the liquor, which he sipped at and which steeled his resolve somewhat. Awanai peered closely at the bottle, seeing only bitter dregs left within, and threw it to the ground with a snort.

"Mr. Perklee spoke to me of . . . of things he saw. Out here. In the night."

"Oh," Awanai said, nodding. "You mean the airships."

"You . . . he spoke to you about them, too?"

"Hell, yes, he did."

Valiantine's head swam. "And . . . do you believe him?"

"Of course, friend," the man said, smiling. "Everything he said is true. I've seen them myself."

Words escaped the lieutenant as he stared into the dark brown eyes of Awanai and silently questioned what he was hearing. Still at a loss to comprehend the validity of anything at all, he sat there silently with his jumbled thoughts. Looking up at the sky, he discovered that it wasn't morning at all, but more like noon.

They drank a little more, saying nothing all the while. Valiantine found the liquor eased his aches and pain, but produced a drowsy feeling in him. Before he knew what was happening, he desired nothing more but to lay down upon the ground and sleep. And, with no warning to his host, he did so.

When he awoke, it was night and Awanai was nowhere to be seen.

Standing, he made his way past the lean-to and toward the lake, looking for the path he could take back to Perklee's cabin. As he searched, it suddenly struck him that something was very wrong.

As if by instinct, he looked up. A yawning pit of utter blackness hung over him.

There were no stars.

So far as Valiantine could tell, it was not cloudy nor was there anything else that should have obscured the stars. Perhaps because of the stupor he still felt from the moonshine, he couldn't understand it.

He looked all around, not only at the sky, but also at the trees and the lake and the ground. Everything was still and quiet— unnaturally quiet, he realized. There was no sound of insects or birds to be heard at all.

This confounded Valiantine. He'd been in many other countries and on different points on the globe, but nothing in his experience gave him a foundation from which to build a hypothesis. It was as if everything in the world surrounding him had come to a complete stop. And because of it, the stars had presumably disappeared. That made no sense whatsoever to his understanding of science and the physical world.

He paused from his visual observation to listen intently for sounds. One came to him, slight and scant. At first he couldn't identify it, but then made it out as the creaking of wood. And nearby.

The lieutenant walked a few paces down the path, straining his ears for the source of the faint sound. All of a sudden, the sharp report of a tree branch snapping sounded overhead, then another.

There were trees all around him; he could not determine which one had produced the sound. Strangely enough, there was not the accompanying noise of a branch falling to the ground. This disquieted him even more.

In a great rush of near-overwhelming awareness, Valiantine felt a great presence above him.

He was not observing the absence of stars, he realized with sickening dread, but the bottom of some impossibly immense *thing* directly overhead.

The lieutenant's first, immediate inclination was to remove himself far from its presence, but in a remarkable feat of self-control he remained where he was and craned his neck to absolutely confirm his impressions of the phenomenon. When the black ceiling over his head proved as inscrutable as when he first divined it, Valiantine made up his mind to find its beginning . . . or its end.

He began to sprint down the path in the direction of the cabin with one cognizant thought running through his brain: *It was right over him!* Later, he would not be proud of the arc of panic and awe he allowed to suffuse his thoughts, but would acknowledge it as a singular event in his life.

Some several yards ahead of him, he saw stars. The thing was truly immense, whatever it might be. And as silent as the grave.

Valiantine came to a stop and wheeled about, trying to comprehend what he was seeing. Here, to one side, was the total black of the thing; there, alongside it, were stars.

He realized he was looking at the edge of the thing. He could just barely make it out, forcing his still-addled brain to comply with the rules of reality he knew for certain still existed when he was secure in mind and body. *Or did they?*

Oh, how he wished he had his pistol on him at that moment.

But why? What would he do with it? Fire it at the thing? Hoping to accomplish what?

To confirm it was real, he told himself.

A queer mirth overtook him: Valiantine wondered with a dry chuckle why he wasn't hearing music, like Perklee. In a strange way he was almost envious of the odd man.

He needed light. He needed to brighten the sky so as to illuminate the thing. Was it a ship? No, he refused to call it that. For now it was simply a *thing*, until he knew more.

Valiantine fumbled in his pocket and brought out a box of matches. He smiled to himself momentarily, remembering the loving teasing of Eileen in Virginia Beach over his particular ways. "Always be prepared," he'd told her on numerous occasions.

A thought struck him. Casting aside the matches and, without any qualms in doing so, yelled up at the thing.

"Hello! Hello the ship!"

It was a leap of faith, labeling it as such, but he reasoned it made little difference at that moment. He cared only to know more of it—to determine if it were real or simply some trick of the atmosphere on his senses.

He found himself running, though he hadn't intended to. He fell, having caught his foot on a rock or a root. Crashing to the ground, Valiantine brought his hands up just at the last moment before his face smashed into a small knot of wiry, thorny brush.

Pulling himself to his feet, he looked up and cursed again and again and again.

He saw only stars, as far as the eye could see, and wondered if he had truly seen anything more.

To pass the time while waiting for the major, Valiantine picked out objects in the man's office and made mental notes as to how he might rearrange them. With a full thirty minutes having passed after being shown into Wellington's office, Valiantine was on edge.

Then, blessedly, the door behind the desk opened and the major appeared. He was still talking with someone—unseen to

Valiantine—in the other room, as if the lieutenant wasn't even there. The gist of it seemed to be assuring the other person that "things would be seen to."

Standing up to salute, Valiantine just wanted the interview to be over with, whatever its outcome.

One eyebrow on Wellington's face rose as he glanced at the lieutenant, standing there saluting. With a practically non-existent nod, the major motioned for him to sit down again.

"Read your report," Wellington said, staring at what Valiantine assumed was the file in question. "You've nothing more to say than that?"

He'd stayed in Manitou a full week after the events of the strange encounter at the lakeside, watching and waiting for signs he hadn't suffered some sort of loss of his faculties from the beating. Perklee never returned to his cabin, nor did Awanai the bandit show his face again, at least not in and around Manitou. There had been a newspaper report of a bank robbery in Fort Wayne, but Valiantine didn't follow up on it. If the criminal had any real connection with the airship, he sensed it to be so minute as to not be worth the trouble of tracking him down.

Later, he regretted not putting the effort into it and wondered at what had become of his normal resolve. The encounter outside the town had apparently shaken him more then he'd realized.

As for Perklee, Valiantine resisted the track on which his thoughts desired to travel, that the man vanished not by the machinations of the citizens of Manitou, but by other, darker forces. It felt too easy an explanation, one which he was not prepared to embrace. Not yet.

From the little town he had made his way to Rochester and then on to Gary, all the way looking for anything odd, any reports of strange occurrences of any stripe, but there were none to be found. Indiana in the spring was much like any other place; there was more to concern people than floating question marks in the skies above them.

He had spent a few days in Chicago, then returned to

Washington. With no real parameters to his orders, Valiantine felt he'd the latitude to move at his own pace, but the tiny voice of compulsion in his head urged him to return to his superiors and make his report in person.

The report came out lacking certain details of his travels, perhaps most importantly the strange phenomenon of the absence of stars. Thinking back over that evening, of Awanai's "hospitality," he could only conclude that he'd been drugged by the bandit. The later situation with the night sky was inconclusive and potentially embarrassing to reveal to his superior. Valiantine had no real proof of what he thought he had seen. None whatsoever.

He countered his own fears of disobeying orders by reminding himself, again, he'd been given little in the way of a finite end-game to the mission. Thus, the lieutenant decided to hold back on describing much of his encounter until he was more certain of what it had actually entailed. Or if it even happened at all.

"No, sir, nothing else," he told Wellington, staring the man down, almost daring him to call him a liar. With his almost spotless service record, it was tantamount to treason to his mind.

The major did stare back, and for several moments. Valiantine detected no malice in it, only some sort of scrutiny that defied categorization.

"Think you'll ever make captain, Valiantine?"

The question took him by surprise. He couldn't begin to imagine what was meant by it.

"With all due respect, sir," he replied, keeping his voice level, "I've no desire to hurry that along. I'm content where I'm at."

"One of the oldest lieutenants we have right now," Wellington noted, unblinking. "Ah, well, that's not my concern, is it?"

The major stood up. "Come with me, Lieutenant."

He arose, tucking his cap under his arm and, brushing off his uniform and straightening out any wrinkles, followed his superior out the door and into the hallway. From Wellington's office they made their way to a staircase and up a flight to the next floor.

"Things are changing, Valiantine," the major said as they

walked. "President's got much on his mind now, but he wants to foster a spirit of cooperation between departments. *All* departments."

The major waved him over to an unmarked door, but paused before opening it.

"There's to be a new venture in town," Wellington said in low tones. "We'll be working with the Treasury boys on a few things."

Valiantine didn't precisely know who "we" were supposed to be, but he let that lie as he pondered the significance of the United States Army working with the Treasury Department. So far as he knew, the Service went after counterfeiters and the like; in fact, they may be interested in his notes on the infamous Indiana Bandit. *Could that be it?* he asked himself. Would he be sent back to the state to run around after Awanai? He could think of much better uses for his abilities . . .

"With that in mind," the major continued, "I have someone for you to meet."

He opened the door onto a plush office, with dark carpets and paintings of sea vessels on the walls. On a small red leather couch off to one side of an immense desk sat a young man, a redhead of medium height and build and of neat appearance. The stranger rose from the couch when Wellington and Valiantine stepped into the room.

"Lieutenant Michael Valiantine, this is Agent Cabot, Treasury Department. Cabot, Valiantine."

The two men shook hands. Valiantine felt the strength in Cabot's grip; firm yet not aggressive. Confused, the lieutenant looked to his superior with a questioning eye.

"Get to know each other," Wellington said. "You'll be working together."

Valiantine frowned. "I'm afraid I don't understand, sir."

The major produced an odd smile.

"Agent Cabot is your new partner, Lieutenant."

BROKEN

Duane Spurlock

June 1897

Rash Howard's only impulsive moment was when he proposed marriage. In all other matters, he was careful and methodical, patient and slow. In this way he faced nature's deviltries and worked a farm outside the community of Broken Toe, Kansas.

Today he drove a wagon pulled by a spotted mule to the home of Mrs. Brecker and her son, Sam. The widow and boy kept a small farm with a few pigs and chickens and a garden big enough to provide for their needs plus excess for selling to neighbors and bartering for goods in Broken Toe.

Five days ago Rash had looked up from sawing a log to see Sam Brecker facing him. The Breckers lived about five miles from the Howards. The ten-year-old had come to tell him his mother had a new milk cow that produced more than the two could use, and the Howards and other neighbors were invited to purchase the overflow.

"Mr. Howard, you never saw such a cow for making milk," Sam gushed. "Ma could probably make enough butter for the whole county if she had the time."

Sam had chattered about the cow. A man had arrived at the Brecker farm with the cow, had convinced Mrs. Brecker to trade her old cow in exchange for the new cow.

Sam's eyes shone. "And he threw in a gold coin, to boot!"

This transaction sounded odd to Rash. But perhaps Sam didn't have all the details straight.

The Brecker homeplace—a soddy dwelling, a sod-and-timber out-building, a fenced-in pig lot—came into sight. Rash knew the widow and her son were pressed to work hard, and the place showed the results: the house and grounds were tidy. Flowers bloomed in the soddy's door yard, and the garden patch behind the house was weed free.

Rash drove the wagon closer.

Something looked wrong.

The pig lot was empty. Not a chicken was in sight. There was no sign of the remarkable cow.

Rash neither hastened nor slowed the mule as he approached. As he pulled up before the soddy, he twisted his neck and surveyed the empty lot and yard.

Rustlers? Rash saw no obvious signs of violence.

The woman and boy—where were they?

Rash listened. The silence seemed unusual on what should have been a working farm. So much so, Rash heard the slight noise of the mule flicking one of its long ears.

"Hello!" he called out. He winced at the sound of his voice cracking the silence.

No response.

Rash stepped to the ground. He hesitated at the door, listening still. He knocked; no response. Then he reached and opened the door.

Rash was not a man who rushed. But he was light on his feet, and if he needed to hurry, he could move quickly.

When Rash saw the interior of the soddy, he whipped around and ran toward the wagon. Fast as he could.

He wasn't fast enough.

When, in the summer of 1800, the capital of the United States moved from Philadelphia to Washington at the direction of President John Adams, only one building in the District of Columbia was ready for use: the Treasury Building.

The building had been the site of much activity since then. It was nearly destroyed by fire within six months of its first occupants' arriving. The British razed it during the War of 1812, and another fire consumed its replacement in 1833. The new building the government eventually constructed was occupied by troops during most of the Civil War. President Andrew Johnson used the site for his offices to allow President Lincoln's widow time to grieve before she moved from the White House.

Such volatile situations were not present this day. Instead, a minor firestorm of rumor swept through a small suite of offices on the second floor.

Three men—each in the neighborhood of the age of thirty years—appeared to busy themselves in the large room that served both as an open office for several desks and as an entry to the inner enclave of their supervisor, Assistant Director Hammond Gallows.

"Cabot's been inside with the Old Man a good quarter of an hour," one said. He had sandy hair over a long, thin face, and his chin appeared to spear his shirt front as he bent over a leather-bound ledger. His gaze moved to the closed door centered in the opposite wall.

One of his fellows responded, "Gallows has reduced more than one dashing young fellow to cinders in less than half that time." This second man was round-faced and red-haired. He did not pretend to work, but stared openly at the door.

"Perhaps," the third said, "he's delivering Cabot his packing papers. Sending him back to the environs of his beloved detective *optimus maximus*, Yankee Bligh." He rolled his eyes, appearing to search for the dark brown hair that had, some point in the past, receded from his forehead. While the voices of the other two men had carried a dash of jocularity, the blade of disdain was sharp in the third man's tone.

A click from the door latch made all three men find sudden interest in the papers before them.

The door opened. After it closed, a young man—a bit

younger than the three men already in the room—moved with a determined stride toward the exit.

The sandy-haired fellow looked up. "Back to work, Cabot?"

The redhead joined in: "Or do you get some time to relax? You only arrived back from Baltimore an hour ago."

"No rest for the weary! And with vitalizing work like ours, who could possibly be weary?" Cabot waved the bowler he carried in his hand, and then hurried out.

The redhead murmured, "He seems very pleased for someone who's been reprimanded."

Sandy Hair nodded. "Back to the field for Cabot."

The third man continued to stare at the doorway after Cabot had dashed through the exit. He said one word: "Drat."

Cabot knew his dusty, travel-wrinkled clothes would not promote a professional appearance to the Police Chief of Broken Toe, Kansas, but he didn't want to delay starting his investigation. He also was aware that to a stranger he would look like a dirty youth in a man's suit and hat, but he hoped his vitality and enthusiasm would win over the gruff-faced man before him.

Cabot advanced toward Barker's desk, hand extended. "Chief Asa Barker? Agent Cabot, United States Treasury Department." Immediately the agent saw that Barker respected federal authority: the chief stood quickly and shook hands. Cabot made sure he returned the firm grip with one of his own.

He knew from experience his boyish face could work against him. Cabot stood about five-eight, hat in hand. Wavy hair something between ginger and auburn, tending more to the darker color. Short nose on a squarish face softened with rounded cheekbones. Blue eyes, lively expressions that matched the briskness of his movements, which he hoped demonstrated a let's-get-to-it quality. Black traveling suit over a gray vest that bore black stripes. White shirt, black cravat. Cabot had been told his enthusiasm for his job could suggest a callow energy, but he intended the look in his eyes to communicate, *I mean business.*

Cabot sat in one of the leather-covered guest chairs at Barker's gesture. He made sure not to kick over the ceramic spittoon placed on the floor for visitors.

Barker returned to his seat. "I'm surprised to see you, Agent Cabot." The young man noted how Barker used his title instead of *Mister*.

"To see me, Chief Barker?" Cabot followed his mentor's lessons in dealing with men who used titles when addressing strangers. Such behavior suggested these men's own titles and positions were important to them, and expected the same in others. And Barker wore a dark blue uniform with brass buttons, something Cabot would expect to see in a metropolitan area, but not on a police chief for a small Kansas town. He noted the matching cap suspended from a hook on the wall behind the desk.

"Well, not you personally," Barker explained. "I didn't know you were coming. But that the Treasury Department would send someone all the way from Washington to Broken Toe is a surprise." He sat forward and knitted his fingers together on the oak desk.

Cabot smiled. The desk was clear except for a pen-and-inkwell stand and a single sheet of paper arranged just an inch beyond Barker's hands. Here was a man who disliked clutter. Cabot extrapolated from the desk's neatness that Police Chief Asa Barker took to heart his responsibility to the electorate to impose order on any potential chaos.

"The Treasury takes very seriously reports of counterfeiting. It is a threat to the stability of our nation's financial underpinnings and to the trust the citizens place in our country."

Barker nodded his understanding. "I know the gravity of my discoveries."

"But," Cabot said, "don't think that simply because you are far from the District of Columbia that your concerns aren't noticed or appreciated." Cabot felt a momentary flash of dizziness, a bit of panic that he might be laying it on a bit too thick. What would his mentor, Yankee, do? *Show confidence,* he'd said, *even if you don't have it.* The advice given Cabot by the former chief of detectives for Louisville, Kentucky, had rarely steered the agent wrong. He swallowed. "You clearly understand the importance of your responsibilities, Chief Barker. Not every man in your position would have wired Washington on finding fake coins."

Barker frowned. "These things are like cockroaches. Come across a few little clues, there might be a lot more behind them."

The Chief looked at his clasped hands, and Cabot wondered if he'd been too hard to judge the man regarding his pride and ego. At the same time, he hoped his worries hadn't been apparent.

Cabot cleared his throat. "Tell me about these coins, Chief Barker."

The chief looked his visitor in the eye. Cabot mentally waved away the phrase he'd read in a dime novel during his train ride: *steely gaze.*

"The coins turned up at the two murder scenes," Barker said.

Time seemed to stop for Cabot. "Murders?"

"Murders," Barker repeated. "Even now, this far from the War of Secession, there are still bushwhacker and jayhawker reprisals between folks from Kansas and Missouri. But those usually have a different character than what we found in these cases."

"And?"

"The bodies," Barker said, then sighed. "They were . . . ripped apart. Like something . . . *wild* had been at them."

"I'm sure there are coyotes and wolves in Kansas," Cabot said. *Were there,* he wondered, *bears?*

"Oh yes," Barker said. "Wild boars, too. Vicious things. Pigs that got loose during the War, went feral. Those animals will mangle a body to a certain point. I've seen plenty of that." He leaned closer, intent. "These people were torn limb from limb. No wild animal I know does that." He sat back. "Over time, animals will pull apart a carcass, spread it around an area. But that's over weeks and months. I once found the bones of a man who'd been missing for a year. They were scattered over an acre." Barker shook his head. "But these folks—these murdered people—were found only a day or two after the crimes."

Cabot watched the chief, and the man—perhaps about forty years old, the agent reckoned—had appeared to grow older as he spoke. Even the brass buttons on Barker's uniform seemed duller.

"We found these coins at the victims' homes." The chief unlocked a drawer on the right side of his desk. He brought a metal box into Cabot's view and placed it atop the desk (but, Cabot noticed, not overlaying the sheet of paper). Barker pulled a key from another pocket, unlocked the box and opened the lid.

He stared at the contents of the box. His lips parted.

Cabot sat forward. His foot rattled the fancy spittoon. He glanced down, a flash of irritation crossed his face, and he looked back at Barker, who hadn't moved. "What is it?"

The chief reached into the box. "The gold coins." He opened his hand to show Cabot two featureless metal slugs. "They're gone."

The Broken Toe police force comprised two men along with Chief Barker—Williams and Walker. They didn't wear uniforms like Barker did, but were dressed alike to enforce the image of their authority: white starched shirt with celluloid collar, and the rest black—bow tie, trousers, cutaway coat, and boots exhibiting a well-tended shine.

Barker raged at his two men for several minutes until Cabot asked a couple of questions. Once it became clear the key—notably, the only key—to the box had never left Barker's possession, the police chief growled and sent the two out of the office. Cabot examined the box. The lock showed no signs of having been forced.

"Can you describe the coins?" Cabot asked.

Barker calmed and got back to business. "They looked alike. Gold coins, not new minted. They'd been passed around for some time. Worn. I thought at first they were double eagles, but the size wasn't quite right. They just didn't look . . . right. I don't claim to know every gold coin that's been struck, but they didn't look familiar. Since they were found at murder scenes, I decided to err on the side of caution and alert the Treasury Department. Just in case they weren't legitimate currency, and if they may have been linked to the killings."

Murders. Even though Cabot had encountered violence in the course of his investigations, none of his counterfeiting cases had involved murders. He could hear his mentor's words in Yankee Bligh's strong, gravelly voice: *Track down every clue.*

"I believe that is sound reasoning, Chief Barker. May I see the bodies?"

Barker gave him an odd look. "They were buried weeks ago. If not, every buzzard in the state would have been circling the sky above Broken Toe."

"Ah, right. Where did you find the coins?"

"At the homes of the . . . victims."

"May I see those?"

Barker nodded. "Do you want to freshen up at the hotel first?"

"I checked my bag when I arrived, but came right over here. I'll be fine. I'd like to look for clues while there is still light."

Barker had assigned Walker to accompany Cabot to the first house. It was a cabin just two miles east of town. It stood company with a fenced lot and an outbuilding on about an acre. The men tied their mounts—Cabot had rented a horse from a livery in Broken Toe—to a fence rail.

In the dooryard, Walker pointed to the shed. "An arm—the right arm—was found against that wall. It was still holding an old Navy Colt." He pointed to the house. "Fired once. We dug the slug out of the wall beside the door." The door was off its hinges, but had been propped back against the frame and nailed in place.

Walker had said little on the ride out except for a grunt or a hum in response to each of Cabot's remarks. The Treasury agent found the policeman's dry recounting a good fit for the personality he'd shown so far. "What else?"

Walker pointed into the fenced lot. "Head and torso in there. Still connected. No cow, of course."

"Why 'of course'?"

"We learned from neighbors that both murder victims had recently bought cows. One cow, each family. The cows were gone when the bodies were found. We think rustlers or somebody—maybe the killer—stole the cows after the murders."

"When did this happen?"

Walker glanced at the cabin's roof line. "Six weeks ago, give or take a day or two. Left leg was found up there."

"And the other murder?"

"Two weeks after that." He gestured with his chin. "Right leg was on the other side of the cow lot. Never found the left arm."

Cabot looked around the lot. "May I go inside?"

Walker didn't answer, but retrieved a claw hammer from a saddle bag on his horse. While Cabot waited, he examined the door. Walker pulled out the few nails holding it in place.

Cabot whistled. "This has been flat-out knocked off the hinges. Look here, the screws pulled out of the door. Wood split against the grain. Latch broken in half. Was the door found in the house or outside?"

The policeman frowned. "In the yard."

Cabot entered. The place had three rooms, and each one was wrecked. Furniture overturned and broken, the stove knocked over, crockery shattered.

"You said a family lived here?"

"Smith and his missus, two boys. Five and nine."

"Smith was the victim?"

"Yes."

"The others?"

Walker shook his head. "Don't know. No one's seen them."

"Since the murder?"

"Boys were at school until two days before the murder. Teacher said they both were ailing, so she wasn't worried when they didn't show up the next couple of days. Best we figure, Smith

45

was killed the day before he was found. Mrs. Smith was at a neighbor's house day before the killing. Trading milk for eggs, so we know the cow was still here then."

"No sign of the wife or boys since?"

"Not a stitch or splinter."

"What about the coin?"

"I found it," Walker said with some pride in his voice. "In a pocket of what was left of Mr. Smith's britches."

Cabot stepped back outside. He paused and didn't move a muscle. He searched for some sign of his mentor's voice in his memory.

Cabot began walking a circle around the cabin. He spiraled around the lot, his circle enlarging as he went counterclockwise, his gaze scouring the ground. Walker watched from the doorway.

Cabot's track eventually took him beyond the outbuilding and fence. He stepped more slowly through the garden plot behind the cabin. "Here," he called. Walker trotted to the agent's side. Cabot plucked a scrap of fabric from a stalk of okra. "Look."

Walker studied a stain on the scrap. "Might be blood."

Cabot pointed to the ground. In the six weeks since the death of its owner, weeds had sprung up in the rows that had gone without a hoe's bite. "You can make out tracks. Deep at the front, like someone running. Away from the house. Maybe Mrs. Smith?"

Walker scanned the ground. "No sign of anyone following."

"Wouldn't have to run through the garden just because you're chasing someone." He nodded toward a wooded area. It was roughly a hundred yards away, and stretched in an irregular line north and south. "What's over there?"

"Creek."

Cabot headed in that direction, continuing to scan the ground. He entered the trees about twenty feet from the creek, Walker trailing. The racket raised by birds in the trees covered the sound of their shoes crackling through leaves and briars and the low-growing plants. At the water's edge, Cabot stopped. The creek was about eight feet at its widest point; according to Walker, it was three at its deepest.

"The water's receded from its highest point." Cabot pointed at the dirt-caked litter along the banks. "When was the last rain?"

Walker examined the gap between the water and the start of the undergrowth. "Some light showers during the past few weeks. Last soaking rain? Maybe two months ago."

"So, right around the time Smith was killed." Cabot began walking north along the creek. He pointed south. "That way— look for prints in the mud."

The Treasury agent soon kneeled. "Here we go." Two marks made by booted feet running in the mud, charging toward the water. Distorted by the force of the runner's movement and the mud's pliability, the marks—now dried and stiff in the area left behind by the dropping water level—still were recognizable to Cabot.

He examined more closely the area to the sides of those prints. And received a shock.

He found another footprint. But much larger, wider than the span of his spread-open hand and nearly as long as his forearm. The foot was unshod—Cabot could hardly imagine a shoe that size—and the great toe actually wasn't in the lead position, but rotated farther to the side, in the way a primate's great toe acts like a thumb.

A brief thrill ran up his neck as an image flashed through his memory: that of the villain from Edgar Allan Poe's story "The Murders in the Rue Morgue."

He shook his head. Perhaps the print had been distorted first by the malleable nature of the wet mud and then by the process of drying.

Just then he caught the sound of Walker calling him over the noise of the birds and of the moving water. He joined the policeman, who had found another print. Like the one Cabot found, this one was grotesquely misshapen, but not so large. Both were pointed toward the water, suggesting each was made by separate people—creatures?—and not by one returning to the banks after venturing into the water.

Two?

Cabot stood. "The other side, then."

He removed his boots and carried them. With Walker's help, he found a way across the creek by stepping on some large stones. On the other side, he resumed sweeping the ground for clues. Several yards to the north, he made a discovery.

He picked up a small dirt-covered boot, a woman's shoe, and waved it for Walker to see. "She must have made it across the water." But search as he might, he found no footprints leading from the creek. None for the woman nor for the strange feet whose prints they'd found on the other bank. He cast about in wider arcs from the spot he found the shoe. After several minutes he paused and considered.

He lifted his gaze, looked into the tree canopy overhead. The leaves swam with birds.

Like a rag doll tossed into the trees, there hung Mrs. Smith, clutched by branches.

What was left of her.

They found no trace of the boys.

Walker urged a return to town. He wanted to send some men out to retrieve Mrs. Smith's body before dark.

They had been riding a few minutes when the policeman said, "I'm surprised we didn't find that shoe the other day."

"May have fallen just recently. The . . . state of decomposition may have caused it to fall after a few days."

Walker nodded as the hurt to his professional pride eased a bit. "Where did you learn to track so? An Injun teach you?"

"No, all I know about investigating crimes I learned from Yankee Bligh."

"Bligh—didn't he nearly catch Jesse James?"

Cabot nodded. "He was quite the policeman. I grew up in Louisville hearing about his exploits. I was inspired to join the police force. I was fortunate to catch his eye and to be mentored in his methods of detection. He encouraged me to strive beyond my career in Louisville, and I was emboldened to seek a position in the Treasury Department."

"Guess that worked out."

"It did. I was very surprised that my desires turned out in my favor. As if a dream too good to be possible came true."

Cabot supposed Walker was about his own age. He saw his companion's brow knotted in thought.

"A good policeman will be welcomed anywhere," Cabot said. "It's still a big country. The law needs good men on its side." Walker looked at him. "You might think about that."

Walker nodded. "I will."

In Broken Toe, Walker directed the undertaker and two recruits to the Smith farm. Then Cabot and the policeman reported to Barker. Afterward Cabot retired to his hotel, sank into a hot tub of soapy water, and finally settled into bed.

The next morning, Walker guided Cabot to the second murder scene. The Smiths had lived two miles east of Broken Toe. The Kellys lived two miles west of town.

The house was little more than a shack. James Kelly, a widower of ten months, had been found in a state similar to that of Smith. His daughter, Dorothy, fourteen years old, had not been found. Walker reminded Cabot the crime had been discovered two weeks after the Smith murders.

The signs of destruction were like those Cabot had studied yesterday. Walker pointed out the places he'd located Kelly's scattered parts. Again, no cow or other livestock had been found at the scene. Barker had been here with him that day, and the Police Chief had found the gold coin with some other money in a broken sugar crock.

The tatters of a ripped-apart dress on the floor of the wrecked kitchen held Cabot's attention for several minutes. He found no strange footprints as he had at the Smith home. After two hours, the Treasury agent gave up looking for further clues.

He collected the reins of his rented horse and asked, "What else can you think of I should know?"

Walker shrugged. "Other than that third scene . . ."

"*Third* scene? A third murder?"

Walker nodded. "You didn't know?"

"Barker only said two."

"These two—the Smiths and Kelly—they're close enough to town the Chief was willing to consider them under his jurisdiction. But Rash Howard was found fifteen miles away, and that's Sheriff Brohm's territory, and he works out of the county seat. Barker let him have that one."

Cabot questioned Walker for whatever information he could pull out. Then the Treasury agent mounted and rode north. Walker headed back to Broken Toe after saying he was sure his boss wouldn't want him tinkering with county business, no matter Washington's interest.

Cabot followed Walker's directions to the Howard home, where he interviewed Mrs. Howard. She wore black and, over that, her widow's grief.

She knew very little. Only what her husband had told her about Samuel Brecker's story involving a remarkable cow and a gold coin.

"I don't know why someone did that to my Rash," the woman said. "He wasn't just killed, he was—was—*destroyed.*" Cabot saw the meek spark that still animated the woman's eyes dull a fraction more. "Mizzus Gaines told me something. She didn't want to, I could tell, but she couldn't keep it from me, either. She said the gossips talk about something—a *thing*, out there running loose in the county. Something like a man, but not. Bigger, on two legs, or four. The people out on the farms, their stock gets spooked at night. If they see anything, they can't make it out in the bad light of the evening. But they find signs in the fields, on the prairies in the morning. Maybe around their barn-lot, and maybe a chicken or a pig is gone missing."

She stopped and peered at Cabot as if hoping to hear him say something that would make sense come back to her world.

Cabot had nothing to offer her. He expressed his condolences, left behind a card with his name and address, and rode his horse toward the Brecker homestead.

Walker's directions were accurate. Cabot followed the same trail Rash Howard had taken the day of his death.

As he rode into the dooryard, the agent felt Walker's absence like an acute pain. He was alone here, where a man had been murdered—torn apart, ripped from life. The woman who lived here with her son—both were missing. The structures that once had been a home imparted a tremendous sense of loss to Cabot. He felt very alone.

And he thought about Mrs. Howard's words. Her description of a monster that wandered the wilderness, terrorized farms, and killed unsuspecting people like her husband—the rise of such tales was normal after the sort of horrible events that had shaken the scattered inhabitants of this community. Not so long ago, this had still been the frontier. Violent death wasn't unknown here; Barker had noted how grudges left from before the War Between the States still broke out among people in this part of the country. But the inexplicable savagery inflicted on the bodies of the murder victims would make anyone wonder if some wild thing still existed hidden yet alongside the works of civilization.

Cabot shook his mind away from this line of thought. From the saddle, he surveyed the scene. He didn't have Walker to point out where Rash Howard's parts had been found, but he knew the man had met a violent end. The particular details about locating limbs weren't really important. That Howard's mule also had been slain and gutted was a point Cabot noted, but didn't dwell upon.

He stepped down from his mount. It was a piebald, the same horse he'd ridden yesterday. He watered the horse and hitched her to a fence rail so she could crop grass while he looked around. Clouds had been filling the sky during his trip from the Howard home, and the light would be failing soon. Best look for clues, then return to town.

Cabot began by walking his methodical spiral, the house at its center. The ground had been scored by the shod feet of horses and men, but no sign remained—if any had been made—of such remarkable prints as those he'd found at the Smith home.

He glanced at the sky. The clouds were thicker, taking on a cobbled look. The breeze was picking up. Cabot had heard about Kansas storms, and this had the appearance of one kicking into action. He stepped toward the sod house.

The door was intact, not like at the Smith and Kelly houses. Intact and latched. Cabot entered. The front door opened into the kitchen. A stench of something rotten filled the room. He covered his mouth and nose with his handkerchief, breathed through that. Tears still came to his eyes.

The sunlight had subsided enough that Cabot needed to locate a lamp. Once lit, he saw the disarray that had marked the Smith and Kelly homes. But some unformed thought fluttered at the back of Cabot's mind. He grabbed at it, impatient, but whatever was just beyond sight of his mind's eye flitted from his grasp.

He focused again on the soddy's interior.

Something was different here. Different from the Smith and Kelly houses.

Tables and chairs overturned, yes. Broken crockery in a pile in a corner.

Cabot felt a tingle behind his eyes.

The center of the room was clear.

The floors of both the Smith and Kelly homes were scattered with the debris of a violent attack: shattered household goods thrown about, underfoot where they had fallen.

Here, anything that might have been flung onto the floor had been pushed to the sides of the room, against the walls. The floors were cleared. Perhaps the sheriff's men had done that?

Why?

Cabot walked the edge of the room, peering at what had been pushed there. He found the source of the heavy, oppressive smell: an enamel pail filled with something pale, its surface a pocked skin. Where the skin met the wall of the bucket, a black ring of mold grew. A crusted dipper lay beside the pail. *Milk from the remarkable cow?* Cabot wondered. He squinted against the burning tears in his eyes to be sure of what he saw: the surface of the milk was moving, apparently stirred from below. Maggots? Or maybe the stinking milk was aging into some sort of volatile cheese.

He ducked through a doorless opening to a second room. Again, whatever had been tossed to the floor had been pushed up against the walls.

Cabot entered the third and last room of the house. The rotten smell wasn't so strong here, but there was another odor. Like in the other rooms, the center of this one was cleared. But something was different here. *What?* He looked about. He returned to the first two rooms. He heard Yankee Bligh's voice resonating in the bones behind his ears: *When you don't know what you're looking for, don't think. Just look.*

So he stood in the first room, then the second, the lamp raised, and just peered about.

In the third room, Cabot let his gaze wander over the walls, along the lines where the walls met the floor.

Then he had it.

No furniture. Nothing broken.

All tables, chairs, utensils—broken and whole—were in the other rooms. In the third room, only linens—clothing, bed clothes, rags—were pushed up against the walls.

And in one corner was a larger pile. Cabot kneeled and examined the tangled quilts and sheets, blankets and emptied flour sacks. The center of the pile had been hollowed out, depressed as by a great weight.

Someone's been sleeping here.

He recognized the odor he'd noticed in this room. It was the mustiness of an unwashed body coming off the linens. Strong. The pile—the bed, Cabot thought—was large enough to encompass someone bigger than the Treasury agent. Really, he decided, someone the size of a small bull.

Someone? Some *thing*?

It came to him: the floors were cleared for walking through the house. Someone had been living here since Rash Howard's murder.

Maybe before. Maybe whoever had been staying here had been Howard's killer.

The Breckers hadn't been seen since a day or two before Howard's body had been found. What if Rash Howard had discovered the murderer in the house and been killed as a result?

Cabot thought about the condition of the bodies—ripped to parts. What kind of person could do that to a human being? What kind of beast?

Something the size of whatever had been sleeping in this pile of linens.

Still kneeling, Cabot shone the lamplight onto the walls just above the nest. Twigs had been driven into the sod to act like nails, and items hung from them: a locket with the photograph of a young woman and a pocket watch on a leather fob. The arrangement on the wall was such that the two could be seen by whomever lay in the tangle of linens.

He took the watch down and looked it over. Whatever engraving had once decorated the case had been worn nearly away by carrying and handling. Cabot pressed the latch so the cover over the crystal opened. Scratched on its inside surface was a name: Tom Brecker.

He examined the locket. No name. A plain young woman, sober-faced. No name or other identifying signs. Mrs. Brecker?

Cabot stood and placed the watch and locket in his jacket pockets. As he did so, his shoe disturbed the edge of the nest, and an object rolled out, glinted in the lamplight.

A coin. Gold.

The Treasury agent held the lamp close and examined his find. As Chief Barker had said, a quick glance might fool someone into thinking it was an old double eagle. And while the surface was worn nearly smooth, Cabot's scrutiny made clear the coin's details weren't quite right. If the two coins Barker had collected were in the same shape as this one, the police chief had a sharp eye to have suspected counterfeiting.

A cry shook Cabot from his reverie. The piebald. The horse had a calm nature, so anything that could frighten her was worth Cabot's worry.

He pocketed the coin, darted to the soddy's door. He opened it a crack and peered out.

The thickening sky had brought an early dusk. In the gathering darkness, Cabot saw the horse rear and pull against the reins, which he had hitched to a fence rail. The piebald continued to squeal in fright.

Was it a wild animal? Or something else?

The thing that had been nesting in the back room and had killed the Breckers and Rash Howard?

The thing—or something like the thing—that had ripped apart Smith and Kelly, and flung Mrs. Smith high into a tree?

Cabot was surprised by an image that flashed in his mind: that of Howard's gutted mule. The Treasury agent hadn't seen the beast, but he'd seen enough animals injured in accidents to imagine the scene.

Cabot flung open the door and dashed to the piebald. He dodged the rearing horse's hooves and loosened the two half-hitches he'd used on the reins, then danced around the skittish beast as he tried to climb up.

The piebald's screams filled Cabot's ears as he grabbed the pommel and pulled himself up. The horse spun, and Cabot saw a hulking figure come around the back corner of the soddy, loping on four long legs, its broad back arched sharply. In the lowering light and the momentary flash from the corner of his eye as he was whipped around, Cabot couldn't catch particular features other than the thing's shape. Then the piebald dug in its hooves and took off.

The reins were loose and ineffective, clutched in the same hands that still clung to the pommel. Cabot had his left foot in a stirrup, the other leg flew free, and he had yet to find his balance and his seat in the saddle. The piebald galloped in maddened fright. Cabot's fear of falling made his blood thunder in his ears.

And he heard something else—a deep-throated roar. From behind, from whatever thing he'd seen near the soddy, from whatever now pursued him.

Cabot couldn't look back. He scrambled, tried to gain purchase and pull himself into the saddle as he was thumped along by the piebald. He was nearly in place, but still off balance, when the horse shied to the right, and Cabot found himself in space, clutching only the reins.

He had been jarred by the floundering ride, but Cabot had enough sense to release the reins so he wouldn't be pulled along by the horse's flight. He tucked into a ball before he slammed into the ground and bounced along for several feet.

Adrenaline-spiked blood thrummed through his limbs, and Cabot scrambled to his feet without feeling the pains that lanced through his body. The piebald's hooves sounded distant already. The Treasury agent dashed forward, spotting against the growing darkness the blacker mass of a wooded area just ahead. He entered the trees and ducked and twisted to avoid the larger branches as they came into sight. Smaller limbs and vines swatted his face and hands as he swam into the dense body of the forest.

He paused in his headlong flight only once to glance back for any sign of pursuit. He didn't see anything, but he heard the crackle of limbs and leaves when the thing—whatever it was—entered the timber. Cabot took off again.

He rushed as best he could for two minutes. Then he slowed and tried to go more carefully and with less noise, but the darkness made taking cautious steps difficult. Cabot leaned his back against the trunk of a large tree. He made an effort to control the rush of his breathing and listened for sounds of pursuit.

He heard them. The crackling, the breaking of deadwood. But whatever was behind him was moving more slowly than it had out in the open.

Cabot looked at the branches above him. He jumped, grabbed a large limb, and pulled up. He began to climb into the tree, moving slowly and reducing noise as best he could. He hoped the sounds of the thing's progress were enough to cover those of Cabot's vertical flight.

Thirty feet above the forest floor he stopped. The thing—Cabot tried to avoid thinking the word *monster*—continued getting closer, though the noise of its passage suggested it was not tracking the Treasury agent directly to his hiding spot.

Cabot still couldn't see what was following him. His tree, and those all around, were beginning to sway in the breeze. The clouds were thicker, and the darkness was complete. He could see no moon, no stars.

He began to hear the creaking of wood. He thought this was from the trees moving in the wind, then felt differently. The wind wasn't so insistent that it could move the trees that much. But the creaking continued and increased.

He felt some sort of presence. A moment of panic had him peering downward, but he saw no sign of his pursuer. And the sounds of pursuit had ceased.

Cabot realized the presence he felt came from *above*.

He looked up. Through the limbs, the sky was a smooth, featureless black.

In that moment a blaze of cold shot along his spine and clutched the back of his neck. He realized those weren't clouds he saw. Something was above the trees. Something *huge*, blotting out any sight of the sky.

The creaking was coming from whatever held itself above him. Perhaps it brushed the treetops, causing the slight sounds. But otherwise, it was silent.

Cabot fought his panic, rejected the urge that pushed him to clamber to the ground. That's where the monster waited.

Cabot heard the creature on the ground moving again. The noises were those of a large figure moving quickly. Away from Cabot's tree, but apparently deeper into the timber.

The creaking increased, followed by the sharp *crack* of large branches shattering. The sounds of crackling, breaking wood grew louder. Cabot heard the roar of his pursuer again—a long, bellowing noise that rose to a shriek as the source of the cry seemed to move from the ground and up through the interlaced branches.

Cabot poured his energies toward peering through the dark to see what was happening to the creature, to get a glimpse of whatever floated above the trees. But a great burst of light blinded him, and the shock nearly tumbled the Treasury agent from his perch. Cabot opened his eyes but saw nothing except flashing blobs of color that danced across his retinas. A deep thump sounded above him, several yards away, and the cries from the beast—whatever it was—ceased.

The clatter of breaking limbs also ended. A rush of wind swayed the treetops. The presence Cabot had felt overhead was gone.

The Treasury agent clutched his tree until his vision improved. He made his way down, moving quickly, in the process tearing his coat and pants and skinning his knuckles. He staggered back to the edge of the timber, adding scrapes and cuts to his face and hands.

At the moment Cabot stepped out from the trees, a blast rocked the air. He saw no flash or blaze of explosives, but he placed the sound as coming from the Brecker soddy. The shock wave rolled through the ground, strong enough to drop Cabot to his knees.

He stood. His knees shook. He made his way back along the path the piebald had carried him earlier—not so long ago, he realized. Cabot's limbs trembled, drained of the adrenaline that had kept him moving during the chase.

When he finally reached what had been the Brecker dooryard, he found only destruction. The soddy dwelling, the sod-and-timber outbuilding, the fenced pig lot—all were flattened into splinters and clods of dirt. Whatever had been inside the house was now shards and dust.

Except for what remained in Cabot's pockets.

He reached, felt the watch, the locket.

And the coin.

There might be clues to be seen in the daylight. Cabot ached with a number of pains, and new ones were making themselves known with each step. But he had no interest in bedding down in this area tonight. And he had no desire to be caught asleep in this vicinity if any of the mysterious *whatevers* came back—the thing that had chased him or the thing that moved through the air.

Cabot turned his back on what had been the Brecker home. It was a long walk to the Widow Howard's door.

The children remained missing.

The adults were all found. Even Mrs. Brecker.

After his long walk back to the Howard place, Cabot slept—*collapsed into an unconscious void,* he thought—in the shed rather than frighten the widow after midnight by appearing beaten and bedraggled at her door. She'd found him there the next morning. In the swamp of her grief, the woman showed no surprise at finding the Treasury agent sleeping beside her Brinly plow.

She'd tended his minor injuries, fed him breakfast, and loaned her remaining mule for him to ride to Broken Toe. He'd returned on another mount—not the piebald—leading the mule.

He'd been accompanied by Walker. Chief Barker had harrumphed at stepping into the county sheriff's business, but had waved Walker out with Cabot and told Williams to send a message to the sheriff about the happenings at the Brecker place.

Cabot and Walker had searched the ruins of the Brecker structures and found nothing of use. Even the pail of rotten milk had disappeared. And the force of the explosion had wiped out any tracks Cabot's pursuer might have made.

But in the timber, they found signs where the creature—the beast—the *thing*—had broken through undergrowth during the chase. Cabot tried not to use the word *monster.* He had no tangible clues and no real description of what he'd encountered, and tagging it with a word like *monster* based on fears fed by the stories he'd heard from Mrs. Howard—well, Yankee Bligh would have said he was being influenced by hearsay, not discovered facts.

Walker pointed out a gap in the tree canopy. Limbs broken, branches shattered—it was about ten feet across. Cabot thought it was the place he'd heard the beast bellowing when the piercing blast of light blinded him.

They also found Mrs. Brecker. Like the other adults, she was rent limb from limb, as if by a raging giant. But she was buried in a shallow grave, not far from the tree Cabot had climbed, and her parts were assembled and arranged in their proper places.

That accounted for all the adults. But the children were still missing.

That bothered Cabot. He stayed in Broken Toe several days. He asked questions. He learned the Smiths were hard, callous people and used their boys roughly. They would strike the boys in public and berate them loudly and at length with coarse language.

James Kelly, a recent widower, had taken solace for his loss from a jug. Gossip whispered, while eyes were averted, suggested he might have been seeking comfort from his fourteen-year-old daughter.

Mrs. Brecker and her son, Sam, doted on one another. She was kind. He was obedient and good-humored.

Cabot reported to Assistant Director Hammond Gallows all he'd learned upon his return to Washington. In his Treasury Department office, Gallows had nodded, and then raised a hand. In the half-circle formed by index finger and thumb was the gold coin Cabot had found in Kansas.

"You can still see the minting date," Gallows said. "1861. There was a plan at the beginning of the War Between the States to strike a limited number of gold coins specifically for trade with foreign powers for material the Union might need during the conflict." He opened a small hinged box made of walnut and lined with green felt. "However, that plan was never carried out." He placed the coin on the felt, closed the lid, and latched the box with a brass clasp. "I'll take charge of this." He placed the box in a drawer of the ornate desk behind which he sat. He shut the drawer and locked it.

Gallows patted the stack of papers of Cabot's report. "This is fine work, Agent Cabot. A decision has been made to change your alignment within the Department. From this moment, you are re-assigned as an operative for the United States Secret Service." Cabot just stared in surprise as Gallows plucked a badge from a waistcoat pocket and placed it on the desk before the young man.

That was the news Cabot had received this morning. Gallows had told him a meeting had been scheduled for Cabot at the War Department. With whom, the Assistant Director didn't say.

Now Cabot sat alone on a leather loveseat in a well-appointed office. Red seemed to be the dominant color scheme for the room, although its paintings and fixtures exhibited nautical themes. *Wouldn't blue and green be more appropriate for a marine setting?*

The door opened. Cabot stood as two men entered. Both were in Army dress. The older of the two strode forward and nodded crisply to Cabot before speaking: "Lieutenant Michael Valiantine, this is Agent William Cabot, of the Secret Service. Cabot, Valiantine."

Cabot extended his hand, and the two men shook.

"Get to know each other," the older officer said. "You'll be working together."

Valiantine gave voice to Cabot's thoughts: "I'm afraid I don't understand, sir."

The major smiled. Cabot detected no warmth in it.

"Agent Cabot is your new partner, Lieutenant."

THE MISTS OF MORNING
Jim Beard

July 1897

R ubbish!"
Lieutenant Michael Valiantine slammed the small metal badge down on the table and sat back. Staring at the object where it lay among the dinner dishes, he wished it every kind of ill.

After a moment, he picked up the badge again and fingered its embossed surface.

"'Aero-Marshal,'" he read aloud. "What in hell is that supposed to mean?"

Agent Cabot leaned forward across the table, wagging his head slowly. "That we're very, very special, I'd wager."

"Or just very foolish," Valiantine added, unsure if the man was being facetious. "It's hard to credit it. The two of us, from different departments, thrust together to form . . . whatever this is." He held up the badge. "I'm not afraid to tell you I don't like it. Not a bit."

The lieutenant glanced over to take in his new companion. He knew Cabot's own badge had already been secured in the agent's wallet, ready to be shown at a moment's notice. Cabot was young, certainly, and capable, no doubt, but Valiantine felt he had much to learn yet about the other agent. He only hoped Cabot was smart enough to never completely trust his superiors;

he himself had lived through many a scrape by relying on himself far more than his orders.

"Do you want to know what I think of it?" Cabot asked, sitting back in his seat and fingering his hat, which sat next to him on the table.

Valiantine nodded somberly. "Absolutely."

"It's a series of tests."

"On that we agree, then."

The lieutenant looked out the window at the landscape hurtling by and wondered how much of his immediate future would be spent traveling on trains. He'd always been indifferent to traveling by rail, but decided he could soon grow to hate it.

They'd been charged not two days before by Major Wellington to make all haste to Detroit, in Michigan. Some inventor there had supposedly announced he'd solved that nagging problem of sustained human flight, and not by balloon. How the major had come by this news he didn't say, but he'd ordered Valiantine and Cabot to go to Detroit, make contact with the inventor, and "see what's what."

"Too much of a coincidence," Wellington had said. "Find out if he has anything to do with the airships. And, if so, bring him in. Quietly."

Valiantine had his doubts as to how quiet they could be about it if the man was demonstrative in his pursuits, so he hoped their target was of the shy, retiring type.

He looked up from rearranging everything on the table to see Cabot staring at him. He'd seen that look of curiosity over his peculiar habits before on others and forced himself to still his hands and concentrate on the situation.

"How do we operate?" Cabot inquired.

"Eh?" Valiantine said. "Oh, I see your meaning. Since it's simply the two of us, my opinion is that there's no need for a 'leader,' if you will. We weren't given orders for any structure to this whole 'Aero-Marshal' business, so let us agree neither one of us is superior to the other. Offer what you have at the time and inform me of what you're doing or will be doing. I promise to do the same. Agreed?"

Cabot nodded earnestly. "Agreed. That suits me. We should also consider setting up a base of operations, something more centralized to the area we'll be covering. We can't be wasting time traipsing back to Washington after every assignment."

Valiantine conceded that it was a good point. Securing his badge in a pocket, he checked his watch. "Cabot, listen: as I said, you're right to feel this is a test we've been given, though if true, Heaven knows why. But we have our orders and shall make the best of it. This business in Detroit with the inventor should go quickly and we'll be on to the next wild goose chase. It won't be the first for me, and probably not the last, so let's just allow it to play out, eh?"

The young agent nodded, picked up his after-dinner brandy, and finished it off. "So, what do you make of it all? The whole 'airship' flap, I mean. Foreign military? Domestic crackpots?"

"Or mass insanity," Valiantine said, smiling slightly under his moustache. He flashed back to the strange evening in Indiana. "That must be added into the equation. Or perhaps it's the sole answer."

He looked out the window again, not wanting to meet his new partner's eyes as his face flushed from the memory of the unfathomable blackness in the sky over Lake Manitou. Valiantine could feel Cabot's gaze upon him, scrutinizing him.

The young man stood up suddenly, dropping his napkin on top of his dishes. "Going to catch a few winks before we arrive, if you don't mind."

The lieutenant nodded and turned to watch Cabot walk toward the door of the dining compartment. The agent spun around to face him before exiting.

"Valiantine, I . . . I know there's something you're not telling me. That's your prerogative, of course. But, I feel as if I understand it, though I don't know what it is. And I hope you come to trust me in time."

He turned to leave. Alone at the table, Valiantine smoothed down his moustache for the hundredth time and contemplated the wrinkles in the tablecloth before him, counting each fold and line.

There was something his companion wasn't telling him, also, something to do with his own experiences and their new status. He felt sure of it. But if he himself wasn't forthcoming about everything, why would he expect anyone else to be?

They hopped an electric railcar not far from the train depot in Detroit and made their way to their target. Valiantine looked around at the city while Cabot filled him in with a few particulars on the man they'd come to see.

"Andrew Carnavon. More an engineer than an inventor, really. Doesn't seem to be a native of Detroit, but we're unsure of where he was born. Kept a low profile in his work 'til now, which is mostly in the carriage trade. Made a few advances in load bearing, structural integrity, that sort of thing. Unmarried, as far as we know, keeps a small staff and has owned his current residence for almost fifteen years."

"That's not much, all told," the lieutenant remarked. "But I guess it will do. Let's assume that he hasn't had much contact with the law, let alone federal agents. Easy does it, until the point where we must insist he cooperate."

The Treasury man nodded. "I'm familiar with such situations. The velvet glove before the cestus."

"Perhaps you should take the lead on this one, then," Valiantine said with a slight smile.

The lieutenant began to point out the various businesses they were passing to his partner. Detroit's diversity of industry and manufacturing astounded him. Since they'd boarded the railcar, they'd passed plants manufacturing bicycles, paint, beer and other spirits, and pharmaceuticals, as well as lumber yards, iron and steel foundries, and what appeared to be a place that produced entire railroad cars.

Over it all hung the smell of tobacco. Cabot informed him that one of the city's major outputs was tobacco products.

"I once heard it called the 'Paris of the West,'" Valiantine said with a smirk. "Can't imagine what they mean by that with all this."

They rode the rest of the way in silence, enjoying the gorgeous early June day and the wide expanse of clear blue sky overhead. Valiantine liked that; you could see anything that was coming with such a sky.

Disembarking from the railcar, they walked roughly a mile to Carnavon's compound. The part of the city upon which they alighted was dirty and rough, occupied by several low buildings and dotted with smokestacks. The two agents passed few people on the streets, but those they did appeared to be tradesmen and laborers, going about their business and taking no real notice of the duo.

We may be able to walk in and walk out of this easily, Valiantine mused to himself. He'd never visited Detroit previously, but so far as he'd seen, the city wasn't going to top his personal list of favorites. The assignment's culmination would help him place it.

They rounded a corner onto the street they sought. Across it and a hundred feet away stood a long wood-slat fence, some six feet high. Beyond it sat a two-story brick building with two large smokestacks standing like sentinels on either side of it. In the middle of the length of fence was a gate. It was closed and pad-locked.

In front of the gate, and spilling out into the cobbled street, a throng of men in suits and hats milled about. In all, Valiantine counted at least twenty of them.

"Reporters," he said grimly. "It had to be reporters."

The duo stood where they'd stopped at the corner of a building across the street from the compound and assessed the small crowd in silence. Valiantine noticed the agitation that flitted about the group and wondered at it. Competition would cause that, of course, but there seemed to be an extra layer of unrest present. He turned to Cabot.

"Word's gotten out, apparently. This will make things more difficult."

"Carnavon doesn't appear to have satisfied their curiosity," Cabot remarked. "Can't really blame him. Nasty creatures."

He appraised Valiantine with a raised eyebrow. "Back entrance?"

"My thought exactly," the lieutenant said.

They turned and walked back the way they came, making a circuit around the block and coming up on its far side. From their new vantage point they could see a small alleyway that bordered Carnavon's place, down which the high wooden fence continued.

Crossing the street quickly yet still casually, they entered the mouth of the alley and made their way down it, looking for another way into the compound.

"I suppose the reporters have already tried this," Valiantine grumbled. He hoped all their missions would not be like this. He could see what was coming: roadblocks and hurdles. The writing was on the wall.

"My guess is that they have," Cabot said, "but perhaps they've been told they must wait outside the main gate."

"There." The lieutenant pointed up ahead of them to a break in the length of fence. Sure enough, when they approached it, they saw it led to a small door in the side of the building. The door was metal, with one window set into it at eye level and darkened with crepe paper.

Valiantine made a mock-graceful gesture at the portal. "After you," he said to the Treasury man. "Nothing ventured, nothing gained."

Cabot strode up to the door and applied a confident knock to it. Behind him, the lieutenant brushed lint off his coat and trousers.

They waited a full minute before knocking again. Finally, the sound of someone approaching the door from inside came to them. A muffled voice called out.

"Front gate! Not going to tell you again!"

Cabot turned his head slightly to Valiantine and nodded, as if to say, *I told you so.*

"Federal agents with credentials," the young agent called out in return. "Please open this door."

After the sound of latches being thrown and a bolt pulled back, the door swung inward and a face materialized from the darkness beyond. It was a bespectacled man, his features sweaty and grimy. He blinked at the two agents, clearly confused.

Both Cabot and Valiantine held up their new badges. The man squinted at them, trying to read the words embossed upon them.

"Department A-13," the Treasury man said soberly. "Aero-Marshals. We'd like to speak to Mr. Carnavon."

"He's not seeing anyone at the moment," the man said with a shake of his head. "I'm sorry, but I have it directly from him."

"And why would that be?" Cabot asked.

"Why," the man said as he blinked convulsively, "he's about to speak, of course!"

Back out on the street, they joined the crowd of reporters, feeling relatively certain they wouldn't stand out much.

Chewing on his distaste for the press, Valiantine discovered one pleasant surprise in the throng: a woman.

Before he could study her comely features beyond a glance or two, a man came out from Carnavon's building and, reaching between the gap between the gates, unlocked the padlock and removed the chains that held the gates in place.

The lieutenant received an even greater surprise when another man stepped away from the building, approached the crowd, and introduced himself as Andrew Carnavon.

"What the hell . . ." Valiantine hissed, and began to move forward, shouldering past a reporter in front of him.

Cabot's hand shot out in the blink of an eye and caught his partner's arm. His grip was tight, but only enough so to force the lieutenant to pause and think.

"Steady, old man," Cabot said. "What's it all about?"

Valiantine's head shot around to glare at him. "I know him. I know the bastard!"

Andrew Carnavon was a dead ringer for Awanai, the Indiana bandit.

The Treasury man did not release his grip on his partner. "Wait a moment. Let him speak."

Carnavon sauntered up to the open gates and stopped, holding up his hands in a gesture to ask for silence. He was dressed in a simple suit with a large, white coat over it. The coat was smudged with oil and grease and other substances.

"I thank you for your interest, gentlemen," he said, raising his voice to be heard, "but I beg you to be patient with me. I regret that I am not yet prepared to make a full accounting of my discoveries."

A collective moan arose from the reporters. They all looked at each other with various degrees of disappointment and disgust.

"I'm sorry, I'm sorry," Carnavon said, frowning. "I . . . might have been a tad . . . premature in my initial release, but I never assumed that it would cause such a stir. Again, I appreciate that you all have a job to perform, but you must indulge me and wait a while longer, if you can."

"What are you on about, Mr. Carnavon?" a voice called out from the throng. Others echoed it.

"Gentlemen, gentlemen, *please* . . ." the engineer pleaded, becoming visually flustered.

One rough-looking fellow stepped forward, brandishing a notepad and well-chewed pencil. "Are you behind the airships, sir?" he asked in a gruff, accusatory voice.

Valiantine and Cabot perked up. The question sizzled in the air around them.

Carnavon smiled. Crossing his arms in front of his chest, he rocked back and forth on his heels.

"I'm not that wealthy," he said.

"What do you mean by that?" the reporter asked, screwing his mouth up in a grimace. "You're smart enough, ain't ya? Got the degrees for it, eh? What's wealth got to do with it?"

The two agents glanced at one another, ensuring the other was listening closely.

Carnavon cleared his throat. "I thank you for the compliment, but please apply some rational thought to it. If these 'airships' are real, and I have my doubts, it would take a great deal of money to make one, let alone the veritable fleet that supposedly haunts the skies above us."

Some of the reporters tittered at that.

"I do believe that the technologies needed for such a craft exist today," the engineer continued, "but no one has yet to pull it all together and make it work . . . work efficiently, that is. So, it would be a combination of both an incredible leap in thinking and a tidy fortune to make it happen. That's not me, gentlemen."

"You say," another pressman called out, "that it's possible, sir. But these things are doing amazing, impossible things in the skies. Silent, deadly silent. And fast, with turns that would rip apart a balloon. Amazing things!"

"Only in that rag you write for, Jack!" one of the man's fellows shouted. The crowd roared with laughter.

Inwardly, Valiantine agreed with the joke; however humorous its intent, it spoke to his growing suspicion that the newspapers were behind much of the airship flap.

"But it all began out west, in California," Carnavon insisted, his face reddening slightly. "No, I assure you that my path is different! If you will just wait and hear what I have to say, when I'm ready, I—"

Overlapping shouted questions suddenly drowned him out. Valiantine bit his tongue so as not to shout them all down and demand the man be heard. To the lieutenant's chagrin, Carnavon spat on the ground, turned on his heel, and marched quickly back to his building. Behind him, his man swung the gates shut again and secured them with the chains and padlock.

The reporters cried foul and surged toward the gates, jeering and mocking the engineer.

"The side door," Cabot said, jerking a thumb toward the alley. Valiantine nodded once and together they flew down the street and into the alleyway.

"You say you know him." The lieutenant noted Cabot had not phrased it as a question.

"Yes," he said as they approached the side door. "You read the report of my last assignment? The trip to Indiana? This Carnavon resembles the man called Awanai, the bandit who has terrorized that state of late. I'd swear in a court of law that it's the same man."

Cabot took a step back. "Then perhaps you should do the talking this time."

After rousing the bespectacled man once more, they waved their badges and demanded to see the engineer.

Within a minute, Carnavon appeared in the doorway.

"Can I help you, gentlemen? My assistant says you represent a federal agency?"

Valiantine made sure the light was good around him, good enough for the man to see him clearly. Up close, there was no doubt in his mind he faced the same bandit who he drank with in the woods, who most likely drugged him. He had the same average build, the sandy-colored hair and short beard, and the Oriental slant to his eyes. The only thing that seemed absent was the patchwork of scars across his forehead.

"You know me, sir?" the army man asked in steady voice.

The engineer leaned forward an inch or so, looking him over.

"No, I don't believe I do. Should I?"

"Dammit—" Cabot caught his arm again and interrupted his partner.

"We have a few questions for you, Mr. Carnavon," Cabot said. "About your discoveries."

The man's temper flared suddenly. "I don't need to answer to you. I don't need to answer to anyone. You'll hear it when everyone else hears it. Good day to you!"

And the metal door slammed shut in their faces.

Taken aback, Valiantine swore under his breath. "Well, I cocked that one up, didn't I?"

Cabot shook his head. "Never mind that. He's definitely

hiding something. He flew into a rage as swiftly as yourself . . . no slight intended, Valiantine."

The lieutenant smiled grimly. "None taken. You were right to restrain me. *Both* times. It won't happen a third."

He began to walk back down the alley, talking.

"We need to expose him and whatever his game is, but we need more information. Here's what we'll do . . ."

Minutes later, the lieutenant stood at the edge of the crowd of reporters outside Carnavon's compound, marveling at their stubbornness and gazing up at the clear blue sky. A breeze had whipped up, but overall it was a beautiful day.

"Are you armed?" he asked his partner, glancing at him. The weight of his own pistol in his pocket provided him with a sense of security.

Cabot patted a pocket on his own coat, his expression serious. "Yes, Mother."

Valiantine resisted the urge to smile at the good-natured ribbing; back in Virginia Beach, Eileen had told him more than once that he tended to be a "mother hen." Was Cabot's barb a sign it was working out with the man? Were they meshing? *Too early to tell*, he thought, but trust itself would not come easy to the partnership. There were too many unanswered questions about it to suit him.

The Treasury man nodded once and slipped away from the crowd, surreptitiously heading back to the alleyway that ran along the side of the compound.

A subtle scent of perfume touched Valiantine's nostrils, making him think once more of Eileen. He turned from watching Cabot's departure to find himself under scrutiny by the woman he had spotted earlier among the reporters. She stood not three feet from him, the ghost of a grin dancing around her appealing cerise lips.

"Starla Ashton," the woman said, extending one gloved hand to him. "You're new."

Valiantine hesitated, mildly surprised by her forwardness, but then grasped her hand briefly with his own.

He told the woman his name was Thomas Vines, a name he'd used on multiple previous occasions in the field. The lie came easily to his tongue; he hoped it meant his abilities had not deserted him, but lay there, just under the surface, waiting to be used.

She was almost as tall as he was, with dirty blonde hair done up in a bun and a small hat of modest design perched on her head. Her skirt and coat were also of unassuming quality, but clean and presentable. Her shoes, what Valiantine could see of them, were scuffed. He reasoned that she did a lot of walking.

"A reporter, Miss Ashton?"

"Yes, indeed," she said, nodding. "With the *Lansing Tribune*." Her eyes never left his face. It made him a bit uncomfortable.

Valiantine told the woman he too worked as a reporter for a small outfit in Columbus, Ohio. Starla Ashton's eyes narrowed ever so slightly at that, but did not lose their twinkle.

"What do you think of it all, Mr. Vines?" She gestured toward Carnavon's front gates. "Do you smell a story?"

"Oh, there's definitely a smell here," he said, crossing his arms. "Just can't quite figure out what it is yet. You?"

"We broke the Lake Michigan story," she told him. "My editor has a feel for these things, thus here I am."

Valiantine admitted to Miss Ashton that he wasn't familiar with the "Lake Michigan story." He could feel his face flush slightly, and silently cursed himself for acting like a schoolboy.

"Oh," she said, raising one hand to her lips and touching them lightly with her fingertips. "Perhaps they don't see our paper in Ohio much. It happened one week ago, near New Buffalo. Made quite a stir along the lakeside, all the way up to Muskegon."

The army man frowned, calling up maps in his head. "New Buffalo? That's near the Indiana line, isn't it?"

Miss Ashton congratulated him on his geography and proceeded to outline the story.

"A woodworker was delivering a chiffonier to a customer late in the day and didn't get back on the road home until after sundown. He and his cart and horse were only about a mile from his house when all of a sudden a strangely intense light shone down on him from up above. The man had a devil of a time soothing his startled horse, but when he did he saw that the light had kept pace with him, still hanging in the night sky over his head. Well, this then startled the man himself, so he urged his horse on and before he knew it, he was hurtling down the path, the odd light never wavering from its, well, pursuit of him, for lack of a better word."

"And how did the fellow end up?" Valiantine asked, engrossed in the tale.

"In the drink," Miss Ashton said. "So intent was he on watching the light keep up with him, he drove himself, his cart, and his horse right into Lake Michigan."

The lieutenant leaned in a bit closer to Miss Ashton, eager to hear more. "And the light? What of it?"

"Flew out over the lake," she said. "As silently as it had come. And more than a half-mile out, the woodworker said it dived suddenly toward the water and then winked out before it broke the surface."

Valiantine digested the story, weighing its properties, especially its proximity to Indiana. The lady reporter cleared her throat and when he looked up at her, saw Miss Ashton was staring over his shoulder at someone.

Behind him stood Cabot, a queer expression on his face.

"Something," the Treasury man said. "You'd better come see."

Far at the back of Andrew Carnavon's compound stood a small shack of antique vintage, but apparent sturdiness. On its door hung a padlock and chain, not unlike that which adorned the property's front gates.

The lieutenant had to climb to the top of a few small wooden crates that stood stacked against the fence that bordered the shack to be able to see the structure. Valiantine swung his gaze back down to his partner, who stood waiting at ground level for his comment.

"So?"

"It's what's inside that matters," Cabot insisted, and disappeared around a nearby corner of the fencing. Coming down off the crates and following him, the lieutenant found Cabot wrenching away a piece of wood from a part of the fence that nestled up against the back of the shack. The agent motioned for him to look through the opening he'd made.

Valiantine leaned in to peer through the opening and coughed suddenly from an odd smell that issued forth from the hole.

"My apologies," Cabot offered. "I should have warned you about that."

The army man could see there was also a hole in the back of the shack through which he could see into its interior. Slivers of light shone into the space between the boards of the walls and through small holes in the roof. Something large sitting on the floor of the shack dominated the space.

"What . . . what *is* that?" he asked Cabot.

"My guess," the Treasury man replied, "is that it's a meteorite of some sort. I've seen them in the Smithsonian collection."

The large, vaguely spherical object's width looked to be more than ten feet across, practically filling the interior of the shack. Only the upper half of it showed; Valiantine assumed if it were as spherical as it appeared, it most likely sat in a hole in the dirt floor of the shack.

His eyes ran back and forth over its dark, pock-marked surface, and he raised a hand to cover his nose and mouth from the strange smell that seemed to emanate from the massive object. It wasn't exactly a bad smell, somewhat sweet actually, but it worked its way into his nostrils and throat, irritating them.

"I concur," he told Cabot after a moment's thought. "I once saw one in a museum in Philadelphia, but it wasn't of this large size. Incredible that it's still intact . . . if it is indeed a meteorite."

His eyes had adjusted somewhat to the light inside the shack, and he realized what he had at first believed to be insects hovering over the rock was in fact wisps of vapor.

"A gas?" he asked Cabot in a hoarse voice. "Produced by the object?"

"Not sure how that could be," his partner said, "but I'd want to get in there, up close, before ruling it out all together."

Valiantine said nothing, but continued to stare through the makeshift opening. Cabot waited a moment before speaking again.

"You're thinking this has something to do with Carnavon's 'discovery,' yes?"

"Indeed," the lieutenant replied. "A superb find, Cabot. Not certain what it means, exactly, but now we have something more to talk to Carnavon about."

As it turned out, the two agents cooled their heels in a hotel room until the next morning, as their target, Andrew Carnavon, was reported as "indisposed" by his man at the side door. This rankled Valiantine, who struggled to tamp down his rush to wrap things up.

As the sun rose on another clear day in Detroit, they marched back to the compound and demanded to see the engineer. Surprisingly, he came immediately to the door, but as red-faced and livid as they'd ever seen a fellow human being.

"What, may I ask, is *this*?" Carnavon shouted, flashing a newspaper in their faces. Cabot's hand shot out and snatched the paper out of his grasp. Together, he and his partner eyed the headline:

ENGINEER UNDER FEDERAL INVESTIGATION
What is Andrew Carnavon Hiding?

Bewildered, Valiantine scanned the article below the bold words and found it described his and Cabot's arrival at the compound and their interest in the old shack out back.

The byline read "Starla Ashton." The newspaper itself was of Detroit origin.

"She lied to me," the lieutenant told Cabot. "She must have followed us and . . . damn!"

Cabot looked at him questioningly. "But how did she know we're government men?"

Valiantine glanced up at Carnavon's man, who, seeing the agent's notice, swiftly disappeared back into the building. His employer still seethed.

"This may ruin everything," he said. "You had no right to poke your noses into my affairs, my property—"

"Our badges give us the right, sir," Cabot said, cutting him off. "We had nothing at all to do with this fish paper's exposé. But that's not important right now. We have questions about the object you have in that shed, and the potential danger of its . . ."

A rustle of newspaper signaled Valiantine's immediate departure from the scene. The Army man left while Cabot was still speaking, striding briskly down the alley and toward the main gates of the compound.

"This isn't done, sir," he heard Cabot tell Carnavon, followed by an angry and inarticulate exclamation from the engineer.

Cabot caught up to his partner, just as he waded into the clutch of reporters and found Starla Ashton. The woman stood with a few others, an open newspaper in her hands, her expression one of pride. Valiantine reached out, grabbed her by the arm and whipped her around to face him.

"What do you think you're playing at?" he asked. "Do you realize that you're interfering in an official investigation?"

Miss Ashton glanced at his hand on her arm and then to his smoldering eyes.

"All's fair in print and war, sir. If you had just been truthful in your cozying up to me, then I—"

Before Valiantine could respond, one of the woman's fellow reporters stepped between the two of them and snatched at the lieutenant's wrist.

"Hands off the lady, Mr. Government Man," the man said, pushing his face up to Valiantine's. "Or I'll do it for you, sure as sure."

Before he knew it, the surly reporter found himself on the ground, rubbing at his smarting jaw. Valiantine stood over him, reaching into his pocket for his pistol and eyeing the others in the crowd. Cabot was at his side in an instant, not mollifying his partner, but poised as if to join the fray.

In lieu of continuing the fight, the lieutenant took out his wallet and showed his badge, turning in a tight half-circle so as to include as many bystanders as possible. When he could see it had been the focal point of many sets of eyes, he secured it away in his coat.

"Consider this a warning to the lot of you," he said, regaining his composure. "We'll brook no more interference in our business here. In fact, I'm ordering you all to disperse. Now."

The mob of reporters began to break up, turning their backs to leave the area. Starla Ashton threw one last acid-laced glare at Valiantine, then departed.

To his credit with the lieutenant, Cabot said nothing. He took off his hat, wiped his forehead with a handkerchief, and returned the hat to his head.

"What's done is done," Cabot said, looking up at the clear sky. "I suggest we get a better look at that rock in the shed after our engineer friend has turned in for the night."

Valiantine nodded mutely and followed him back to the hotel.

Valiantine set his fists on his hips and appraised his partner in the darkened alleyway. Cabot had taken his handkerchief and tied it around his face, covering his nose and mouth.

"God," Valiantine said, "you look like something out of a dime novel."

Cabot shrugged. "In the Treasury we usually just knocked on doors and announced ourselves. Sneaking around is your strong suit, not mine."

The man's words stung a bit, in light of the gaffe over the newspaper article, but Valiantine offered no rejoinder, simply took out his own handkerchief and tied it around his face.

Besides, he thought, they weren't trying to remain covert, not really, but to save themselves from breathing in any more of the fumes in the shack.

One after the other, they made their way over the fence and up to the door of the old structure. Pausing a moment, they watched and listened for any signs they'd been heard, but when none came Valiantine picked the padlock on the door.

Stepping inside the shack, they closed the door behind them and looked out over the immense object.

"Match?" Cabot suggested.

"No, I wouldn't if I were you," the lieutenant said, stepping closer to the giant rock. "Vapors, remember? Wellington won't care for it if we blow ourselves up."

They allowed their eyes to further adjust to the darkness. Valiantine stood and peered at the object while Cabot made a slow orbit around it.

"Whatever the gas or vapor is, it's definitely coming from the rock itself."

The lieutenant grunted his agreement with Cabot's assessment, and crouched down to get a closer look. Reaching out with one hand, he moved in slowly to touch the craggy surface.

"Be careful!" Cabot hissed, his eyes widening over his hand-kerchief.

"Yes, Mother."

Upon closer inspection, Valiantine could see the wisps of vapor floating up from the rock's exterior, and hanging mere inches in the air above it. It might have been a trick of the dark, but he swore the wisps radiated a barely imperceptible illumination.

His fingers came into contact with the object and found its surface to be cold and clammy.

"Hmm, did you say something?" he asked Cabot. The man did not reply.

Valiantine looked up from his scrutiny of the rock and discovered he was quite alone in the shack.

Light sifted in through the cracks between the boards, as if someone outside the shack walked past it with a lantern or torch. Whoever it was, he made no sound.

The floor began to tilt. Valiantine had a wild thought that the presumed meteorite might tumble out of its hole and break apart against the wall.

The light from outside illuminated the vapors inside. Suddenly, they seemed to be more heavily present. Suddenly light-headed, he wondered if it might not be nitrous oxide, but the idea slipped away as swiftly as it had come to him.

He tried to call out for Cabot, but his tongue felt thick and furred. He could not speak.

With a gasp of realization, he felt no ground beneath his feet. The roof of the shack was only inches from his face.

More light sliced in through the boards, marking multiple sources. The boards seemed transparent, as if they formed only the ghost of a shack.

Valiantine saw figures all around the structure. They moved back and forth around the perimeter like wraiths. He could not count them all, but guessed there to be at least a dozen of them.

Panic gripped his body, his mind. He tried again to speak. Then he tried to scream.

Something gave way, like the gates of a sluice.

As if on a wave, he rode the tide out of the shack and into the open air.

The first light of morning woke the army man. He found himself face down in the dirt outside the shack with Cabot lying a few feet away from him, but face up.

The Treasury Man sat up quickly, looking around for his hat. Valiantine cursed under his breath, then more loudly as he began to pick himself up off the ground. His suit was a mess, and he wiped at it uselessly with his fingers.

"Gas," Cabot said with slurred tongue. "Hallucinations. Mob must have come back to scare us or—"

"You were there?" Valiantine asked, incredulously. "I thought you had left!"

"Yes, dammit, I was there. Why would you think I would leave?"

The lieutenant had no answer for that, but the feeling of being deserted hung on him like lead weights. A remonstration hung on the tip of his tongue, but instead he gave up on his suit and looked up at their surroundings.

"Good Lord . . ."

Cabot glanced up at the morning that greeted them.

A thick mist or fog clung to everything around them, save for their immediate area. Yellowish-gray, it obscured the trees, the buildings, and the fence. Even the shack was faint to their eyes.

Valiantine had never seen a fog so thick, so cloying. Above them and to the east, the sun tried vainly to break through, but offered only a pale, ghostly light. Somewhere, off in the distance, he could hear the clanging of a bell, echoing around the strange atmosphere of the neighborhood.

"What now?" Cabot asked.

The lieutenant swiveled his head around, looking for the fence they'd scaled the night before. Still woozy from the vapors and disturbed by the mists of the morning, he spat at the ground.

"Let's find Carnavon. He has some answering to do for that rock in there."

They made their way over the fence and down the alleyway to the street. The fog shouldered its way in, making them doubt their sense of direction. Finally, they stumbled out into the street and looked around, trying to find points of reference.

The crowd of reporters had returned to the engineer's front gates. Their silhouettes in the mists reminded Valiantine of the figures outside the shack, and he felt his anger begin to rise up and through him.

"We told them to disp—"

Cabot grabbed his coat sleeve, pulling him back. "Look!" he shouted, pointing upward.

Large, dark shapes floated in the fog above them, drifting on straight paths, but on different trajectories. They made no sound.

Valiantine rubbed at his eyes, trying to clear them. The shapes remained. It was like looking up through water at the hulls of immense sailing vessels in the sky.

He glanced at the reporters; none of them seemed to have noticed the phenomenon.

He took a step, but before he could complete it he was rocked back on his heel by a bone-crushing detonation somewhere above him.

Another burst immediately following the first shook the entire area, buildings and all. A fiery explosion some yards from them nearly knocked them to the ground.

Carnavon's laboratory and offices blew apart in the fog.

Valiantine recognized it instantly as cannon fire.

There was no mistaking it; in fact, the distinct sound of it was etched into every fiber of his being after his accident at the fort a year earlier. He vibrated from its deep bass expulsion, once again feeling the dread of its voice and the impact on his body.

People started screaming. A few ran past the two agents, fleeing the scene. The lieutenant looked up to the sky once more, practically frozen to the spot, a witness to the incomprehensible violence raining down around him.

Multiple cannon bursts sounded. Buildings exploded. The whistling arcs of cannonballs joined with the explosions to create a surreal tableau, one that should not, could not exist to Valiantine's way of thinking.

The dark shapes in the sky continued to move back and forth, undefined, but damning in their sowing the seeds of destruction.

Finally uprooting himself, Valiantine raced past Cabot and toward the alley. His partner shouted after him, but he ignored the Treasury man and kept running.

The fog grew heavier, mingled with the smoke from the

collapsed buildings. Behind him, the lieutenant heard the report of a pistol and turned to see Cabot pointing his Smith & Wesson .32 at the shapes in the sky and discharging it.

The cannon fire stopped. A strange, pregnant silence hung in the air. He could just make out the sounds of wailing somewhere out on the street. This brought him up quick, and he turned back to try and find the source of the cries. There, on the street, under the ruins of the large fence around the engineer's property, he found Starla Ashton.

The reporter lay there, broken and bleeding, shards of wood stuck in her at various points on her body. Her dead eyes stared up at the looming shapes in the foggy skies.

A man who appeared to be the same reporter who came to her defense against Valiantine kneeled by her side, holding her cold hand and wailing. Suffused with discordant feelings, the lieutenant offered no help or comfort to the man, only stood by and witnessed the little scene.

The cannon fire had not begun anew. He turned away from Miss Ashton's body and trudged back down the street toward the mouth of the alley, having no idea whatsoever what had become of Cabot. He half-expected to come across the Treasury man's torn-apart body in the street.

A figure walked out of the fog before him, from out of the alley. Valiantine peered through the cloying mists to discern its identity. With a start, he saw it was Awanai, the Indiana bandit.

He knew for certain it was not Andrew Carnavon, but the man with whom he'd shared moonshine along the shore of an Indiana lake. Fury sprouted within him as he saw the way the man sauntered away from the destruction of the compound, seemingly without a care in the world.

Valiantine also at first thought the man had floated out of the alleyway, but dispensed the thought as a product of the mists.

Operating on raw instinct, he pulled his pistol from his pocket and fired at the bandit.

The cannon fire started again a split second later.

Valiantine's shot shattered against the wall of a neighboring building. The army man cursed his poor aim as the bandit looked over at his assailant, narrowing his eyes as if to make him out. Then, he simply disappeared into the fog.

Explosions set fire to the air all around the lieutenant. He looked up to see an entire brick wall falling toward him, over him. Someone bellowed his name and something caught him around the waist, yanking him backward and to the hard ground. The back of his head smacked the dirt and he saw stars.

Bricks bounced off him, hitting his shoes and legs. Valiantine lay back and wished for it all to stop. Just stop. Once and for all.

Then, he passed out.

"Carnavon?"

"Dead."

"His compound?"

"Almost completely destroyed."

"And the shack?"

"Utterly obliterated."

Lieutenant Michael Valiantine lounged on a small settee in the lobby of the Detroit hotel at which they'd made a temporary headquarters. His head hurt. No, that wasn't entirely correct. Everything hurt, every inch of him.

"How do they explain the destruction?" he asked Cabot, fingering a large welt on his head.

The Treasury man reached up to push back a nonexistent hat and rubbed at his forehead instead.

"Lost my favorite hat. Anyway, the local authorities have made a 'preliminary deduction' that the explosions were caused by either a faulty boiler or 'unidentified chemical compounds' of Carnavon's."

"But we know better," Valiantine said, staring at his partner with cold eyes.

Cabot furrowed his brow and frowned. "Do we? Do we actually know better?"

Valiantine sucked in breath and let it all out again in a mighty sigh.

"You comported yourself well," he told the younger man. "And you saved my life. I'm very grateful for that."

Cabot paced back and forth before him. "You would have done the same for me. Think nothing of it."

In reality, Valiantine thought much of it. In fact, he decided there and then, the entire situation with the Treasury man could not continue as it had. The sighting of Awanai, his uncanny resemblance to the engineer, the supposed meteorite, the shapes in the sky themselves—every bit of it demanded more than one mind on the job to sift through their meaning.

"Cabot," he began, "on the train, you said you knew there was something I wasn't telling you. You were correct in that assessment."

His partner raised one eyebrow, pausing in his pacing.

"Sit down, man. I have a story to tell you about an item or two I may have left out of the report on my Indiana mission.

"You've earned it."

GRACE FOR THE DEAD
Duane Spurlock

August 1897

Cabot had gained a partner only recently, but he already understood this sign: when a furrow appeared at the top of Valiantine's nose, he was not happy.

The lieutenant said, "We can hardly go about our campaign without attracting undue attention if we present ourselves immediately to the Chief of Police."

"We would soon be found out and invited to visit the chief," Cabot answered. "I am known here."

Here was Louisville, Kentucky.

The town had been Cabot's home before he went east to seek employment with the Federal government. What he had learned on the police force in this city that bustled on the southern banks of the Ohio River had prepared him for the challenges he met in the capital on the Potomac.

"This is a sprawling river port," Valiantine said. "How well can you be known here?"

"I am known by men on the police force," Cabot said, "and once I am seen by a member of that department, or my presence is remarked to one of them, the chief will know soon enough. So we will begin there."

"We *will?*" Cabot noted the ring of unyielding iron in the lieutenant's voice. "*Should* we, however?"

"We will."

After establishing a makeshift headquarters in Dayton, Ohio, the two had traveled south at the direction of their superiors. They now stepped off the ferry that brought them across the river onto the city wharf and began striding up a cobbled slope toward the backside of the buildings that lined Main Street, which paralleled the Ohio. Cabot caught the attention of a youngster, directed him to deliver their bags to a hotel, and dropped some coins in the boy's hand.

The lieutenant had recommended taking the train all the way to the Louisville depot. Instead, Cabot had them leave the train to cross the river by ferry. "You learn a lot from boatmen," he'd said. And they had learned something: they had overheard some of the crew talking about strange lights appearing in the sky over the river.

Riverside business made a lively scene at midafternoon. Mules and horses pulled wagons loaded with hogsheads filled with tobacco, salted meats, and more. Animals and humans brayed, shouted, and clattered about between bales of hemp and stacked crates of farm implements.

Reaching the street, Cabot continued to stride purposefully along.

Valiantine protested: "Can't we ride there?"

The youthfulness of Cabot's features had melted away, replaced by a focused scowl. A glance at his face made others step out of his way. "I have been gone from here long enough that I need to learn what has changed. I can best do this afoot." Not far from their present location, Yankee Bligh had taught Cabot this lesson: *Ride about town and you'll know the flow of the buildings. Walk a town's streets and you'll know your way around like the ones who live there.*

He slowed just enough to speak a conciliatory word to Valiantine: "I guess I look something like a hound at work."

"No, your nose and tail are both too short."

Cabot almost smiled.

Soon enough, the two stood in the office of Thomas Taylor, Chief of the Department of Police for the City of Louisville.

His nose was red, his forehead high, his hair and mustache thick and dark brown. His eyes lacked humor.

Taylor stood before his black desk and did not invite his visitors to sit.

"Cabot, I've not seen you since you left the department. Has our nation's capital come to bore you? You've returned home to seek more excitement? Or has the District of Columbia simply tired of you?"

Cabot smiled. "I've come here as part of an investigation." He gestured. "Chief Taylor, my partner, Agent Valiantine."

Taylor did not extend a hand, but offered a curt nod. Valiantine made an even slighter nod.

The chief returned his gaze to Cabot. "I know you work for the Treasury. Are you here about the coins?"

Surprise tightened Cabot's chest. Remembering the dangers he'd encountered while tracking down coins in Kansas ran a cold thrill along his ribs. He cleared his throat before speaking. "Coins?"

Taylor's face did not change expression. And he did not answer immediately. When he spoke, his voice carried no hint of what he was thinking. "Yes. Gold coins. Three. They were found by a watchman near the Canal. He turned them over to his supervisor, who notified the department. Gold coins are rarely left behind on the ground without someone missing them at some point."

Cabot asked, "Has anyone reported them missing?"

"Not yet. But I don't recognize them. I'll see you get a look at them before you leave. Perhaps your work with the Treasury will allow you to identify their origin."

The chief paused. He didn't blink as he stared at Cabot. He said, "The coins were found only yesterday. To be here now, you must already have been on your way to town before then. So apparently some other reason has brought you to my office. Why are you here?"

Cabot held his breath a moment before answering. He

remembered Yankee Bligh once saying, *When you have questions, try to control the meeting as best you can. If you can't control the meeting, control your answers.* He'd had no control over this encounter—Chief Taylor had the advantage today. Cabot made sure his expression didn't give away a clue to his frustration. Still, he had unexpectedly learned about some mysterious coins, so perhaps the meeting hadn't gotten completely out of hand.

"We're investigating reports," he finally said, "of things people have seen in the air."

"In the air?" Taylor blinked. He looked at Valiantine, then back to Cabot. "Like balloons?"

"I rely upon your professional discretion," Cabot said. Taylor responded by lifting his chin, and he appeared more attentive. Cabot continued: "No, not balloons, but something large. Like a boat, you might say. But not with the river as its home. Instead, the air."

Chief Taylor's gaze again went from one visitor to the other. "That's preposterous."

Cabot made a slight gesture. "There are reports. We are investigating them. You have not heard of them?" He knew this type of question could work against his wishes: Taylor's pride might be offended by the suggestion that his knowledge about the city—the leverage for much of his authority—might be lacking.

"I've heard gossip," Taylor admitted, "fanciful tales from fools too drunk to keep from tumbling into the street from the saloon door. You've actually come here to chase such phantasms?"

Yankee Bligh: *When you're telling someone something he doesn't want to accept, use familiar, comforting words.*

"We're investigating reports," Cabot said. "We have done so in other towns. We're doing so here."

Cabot waited, expectant.

Taylor's eyes narrowed. "I see."

"Your welcome home has been less than warm," Valiantine said.

They were overdue a meal, so Cabot led the way to a chop house after leaving Police Headquarters.

Cabot spread his hands. "Louisville was settled by clannish immigrants. That still influences the local culture. If you leave your place—your family, your employer, your proper station—it's viewed as a sort of betrayal. The locals would say by leaving for the Treasury Department, I was 'getting above my raisings.'"

"Know your place and be satisfied with it."

"Right." Cabot drank his coffee. "Things with Taylor could have gone better, but we still learned a bit."

The lieutenant chewed and spoke: "He let us see the coins. What is their significance, anyway?"

"Before we were partnered, I was sent to Kansas to investigate a possible counterfeiting case. Two coins disappeared. I recovered a third. Similar to what Taylor allowed us to see in the police vault: gold, very worn, mint dates of 1861 and 1862. The design looked slightly different from what I found in Kansas."

"So? What have they to do with our investigation?"

Cabot looked down at his plate. "While there, I encountered something. I didn't know what it was. But from what I've learned since we began working together, it's clear it was an airship. The one—or one of those—we're looking for."

When Cabot looked up, Valiantine's eyes were shining. "The coins are connected to the airships?"

Cabot held his fork above his plate. "I have no clear evidence they are linked. But I have a hunch. Unscientific, but if coins like these make an appearance in two airship locations, the fact shouldn't be dismissed out of hand." He waved his fork, and Valiantine dodged a glob of gravy. "We know something else: Chief Taylor put no credence in the airship reports. But someone does. The report got to our superiors from some source. If not Taylor, who sent the news?"

"Indeed." Valiantine pushed away his cleaned plate while Cabot emptied his coffee mug. "Now where?"

"The Portland Canal. I'm intrigued by the honesty of a watchman who would find gold and hand it over to someone else."

വ വ വ

The only obstruction to traffic on the Ohio River from Pittsburgh to the Gulf of Mexico were the falls near which Louisville was founded. Providing portage for cargo had been a booming business locally for generations.

"Politics and national economic needs for uninterrupted commerce led to building the canal around the Falls of the Ohio," Cabot explained.

"I suppose local businesses that profited from portage fees weren't very happy," Valiantine commented.

The third man who stood alongside the two agents answered, "Exactly." The three peered out a large window of a block structure overlooking the locks that allowed craft to navigate through the Portland Canal and avoid the falls. Currently a stern-wheeled packet sat in the locks while the water level fell for it to continue its trip downriver.

The tall, gaunt man beside Cabot said, "That's the *Tennessee*, built over at the Howard Boat Yard across the river." He was Delbert Bontonne, Commissioner of the Locks for the canal. He wore a dark uniform with brass buttons. His stiff cap bore the insignia of his office. Bushy side whiskers offset the thin appearance of his long face.

"Commissioner Bontonne, we understand one of your watchmen turned in gold coins he found near the canal."

Bontonne gave the agents a sharp glance. "Oh, I turned those coins over to the police, and I received them, yes. But not from one of my canal guards."

Cabot frowned. "No?"

"No." Bontonne's right hand rose and fingered his gray whiskers. "He was a stranger to me. A man in uniform. I thought at first he was a policeman, but his dress appeared more military."

Valiantine asked, "Did he have a rank?"

"Again, no. No stripes, no braid, no ribbons or badges. So I may have been incorrect in my assumption, but he carried himself very precisely, and the cut of his clothes reminded me of a uniform.

Perhaps he had recently left the Army and still wore his uniform, but had removed anything that displayed his rank."

The lieutenant asked, "What color was the uniform?"

"Black, or nearly so," Bontonne answered. "Coat and trousers both."

"Did he say anything about the coins?" Cabot asked.

"Only that he had found them near the canal, on the path that runs to the east from here. Said perhaps someone had lost the coins and might be looking for them."

Cabot and Valiantine made their way to the place the stranger said the coins had been found.

The path was not tended—just hard-packed earth along the top of a weedy levee overlooking the canal. A tangle of trees and wild grape vines edged the south side of the earthworks, separating it from the streets and structures of Portland, the mercantile and residential foundation of the town as it was originally developed before the city sprawled to the east into what was now named Louisville.

Using markers along the riverside as guides, the agents stopped at the point of the path Bontonne had described.

Valiantine glanced about while Cabot spiraled around the area, wading through knee-high grasses and briars. The sunlight flashed off the water. The humidity beaded sweat on the lieutenant's face. Cabot heard a note of irritation in his partner's voice: "There's nothing here."

Cabot nodded. "If ever there were. I wonder if the stranger gave the commissioner the coins from his own pocket, and fabricated the story of finding them?" He cautioned himself from saying more when he heard Yankee Bligh's voice: *Don't make theories and look for proof. Look for clues and build your case from what you find.* "What do you think about what we heard on the ferry? About strange lights over the river?"

"One said he was reminded of the 1870 tornadoes. After he drank from his flask."

"Something must be going on for Assistant Director Gallows to send us here."

Valiantine planted his fists on his hips. "Now what, Cabot?"

Cabot swabbed his face with his handkerchief. "Now I need a new hat."

The painted sign over the door had not changed since Cabot had left Louisville for the District of Columbia: JOSEPH TAUSTINE ~ HABERDASHER. The Main Street store sat not far from the wharf. The back of the building faced the river.

Valiantine followed Cabot into the store. A bald man wearing pince nez, crisply dressed despite his stoutness, bustled forward to meet them. "My goodness, is that Mr. Cabot after all this time?"

"Indeed, Mr. Taustine. Good to see you again." Cabot introduced his partner, and Taustine shook hands vigorously with both men.

"I need a new hat," Cabot said. He soon was viewing his reflection under a high-crowned bowler. He asked, "Mr. Taustine, have you heard anything about strange events around the river?"

Taustine's lips moved as if he were shifting a cud inside his mouth. He frowned at the floor. "I must say I haven't, Mr. Cabot. Gossip from the businessmen along the river usually makes its way here when they need something for the wardrobe. But I haven't heard anything out of the ordinary. Have you any details you may share?"

"No, Mr. Taustine, but I think you'll know immediately if you hear the sort of thing I'm seeking. You may find me at The Phoenix. I'll just take this hat, please."

"Excellent!"

Back on the street, Cabot adjusted the tilt of his hat. Valiantine sighed and said, "You really put hope in getting information from him?"

"He's excellent for details. He remembered my hat size after two years, you'll note. And he's right about the professional men who visit his store: they are marvelous gossips."

"Now?"

"Now we go to the corner, follow the alley and go to the back of the shop."

At the rear of the building, Cabot knocked on a paneled wood door painted blue. A small sign beside the door read, DELIVERIES ~ TAUSTINE ~ HABERDASHER.

The door opened to reveal a slender Negro. The gray in his short hair and the many wrinkles curving from the corners of his eyes revealed he was older than his visitors, but he radiated a great vitality. He wore a blue chambray smock over canvas trousers. His mouth opened in a wide grin. "My goodness, it's Mr. Cabot! It's quite the day to see you again, sir."

"And you, too, Mr. Bibb." The two shook hands. "This is my partner, Agent Michael Valiantine. Allow me to introduce Mr. Richard Dean Bibb."

Bibb invited them in and shut the door. Here was a tailor's workroom, with all the requirements for the needle trade: three forms for fitting suits and shirts, tape measures, racks of spooled thread, yards of fabric, and prickly pin cushions. "I'm sorry, I don't have enough chairs."

"No chairs are necessary, Mr. Bibb," Cabot said. He turned to the lieutenant. "Mr. Taustine hears news from businesses on Main Street and south. Mr. Bibb creates the clothes Mr. Taustine's customers order, and sews and does repairs for the people working on the wharf and the boat crews. He hears everything of interest anyone would want to know about the river."

"That's still true today," Bibb said.

"I thought so." Cabot asked Bibb if he'd heard strange news from his river customers.

Bibb nodded. "I have heard men talking about lights and noises over the river at nights. Always cloudy or no moon when this happens, so nobody sees anything that explains what they see or hear. 'Comets,' one fellow told me. Someone else said it's the ghosts from Corn Island."

Valiantine asked, "Corn Island?"

"George Rogers Clark established a military settlement there during the American Revolution," Cabot explained. "The settlement eventually grew into Louisville. Over time the river flooded the island and it disappeared."

After Cabot requested Bibb to keep his ears open and gave the name of the agents' hotel, the visitors departed. Back on Main Street, Valiantine asked, "What's next?"

Cabot smiled. "I must apologize. I've taken charge since we've been here. You probably are quite insulted in how little I've included you as a true partner."

"No," Valiantine said. "This is your town. I've been watching you operate in it. You have a wealth of resources—knowledge, connections—that I have little to add to. It makes sense for you to lead the way. You are familiar with the territory."

"Very well. With your allowance, we'll make one more stop before we dine and retire to our hotel."

"And that stop?"

"A new hat requires another accessory." Cabot patted his coat pocket. It held the Smith and Wesson pistol he'd carried since the agents' previous investigation.

Cabot led Valiantine to a storefront on West Jefferson. The painted sign over its door read, SEBASTIAN KONZ ~ GUNSMITH.

Inside, Cabot was greeted warmly by the proprietor, to whom he introduced his partner. The round-faced gunsmith had thick yellow hair and a drooping mustache that hid his mouth. His yellow-and-brown plaid vest carried dark stains. He was a sturdy-looking fellow, but his hands appeared delicate. Shaking hands with him quickly put that notion to rest.

Konz asked Cabot, "You'll want that item you mentioned in your letter, Billy?"

"Yes, Sebastian."

"I have it ready."

Cabot removed his coat so the gunsmith could fit him with a leather shoulder holster. He made some adjustments, then helped the agent put on his coat. "How does it feel?"

"Not bad," Cabot said. "A little close here." He patted his armpit. "But Mr. Bibb can fix that, I'm sure."

"Now," Konz said, "you'll need a revolver for that rig."

While he pulled out from display cases three pistols for Cabot to handle, the agent asked, "Have you had any large orders for rifles? Military grade, not for personal use. Or heard of anyone receiving such an order?"

Konz paused in handing Cabot one of the guns. "No, not that I can think of. How large?"

"Anything out of the ordinary. More than you would expect just a family to order."

"No," Konz said. "I sold an order for six Belgian shotguns for the New Albany Hunt Club about eight months ago. But nothing since then. And I haven't heard of anything from the other gun shops. Sometimes we help each other fill a large order like that if we have it in stock. And any other sort of large order would get talked about at some point. No, Billy, I'm sorry."

"No, Sebastian, no need to be sorry. Just following a hunch." He hefted each pistol in turn, practiced aiming at an elk's head mounted on the back wall of the store. "This one has a nice weight."

"That's a nice little Colt's Single Action Army revolver. Also called the Sheriff's Model. The balance is a little different than your typical sidearm, because the barrel is only three and a half inches long. It will fit fine in that shoulder rig, but you better practice pulling and shooting it. Also, with the shorter barrel, there's no ejector pin. So you can't reload quickly—you have to pull out each empty cartridge."

"Okay."

"You may want to carry another handgun—if you need to reload but don't have the time."

Cabot heard Valiantine clear his throat. The lieutenant said, "You're trading one gun for two."

Cabot looked at the Colt in his hand and hefted it. "I'll stick with this. I have a pocket gun if I need it. But I'll need some shells."

Leaving the gunsmith, the two agents started walking toward

their hotel. Valiantine asked, "You think someone is stockpiling an arsenal?"

"No. But it's worth asking the question. Louisville was officially a Union town, but there were plenty of Rebel sympathizers here during the war. An entire network of spies, too. Yankee Bligh broke up more than one ring of spies and assassins."

Cabot saw a frown furrow the lieutenant's brow. "You think this is a plot to raise the Confederacy?"

The younger agent sighed heavily. "No. I don't know. Yankee Bligh would say I should let the case grow out of the clues instead of spinning possibilities. He'd say, 'You're putting the cart before the horse.' He'd be right. But the dates on the coins, a stranger in uniform—it makes me wonder. And a plot to wreck the Portland Canal could be devastating to local businesses and river traffic all along the Ohio. And the Mississppi." He glanced at his partner. "What do you think?"

Valiantine continued to frown. "It's worth considering. Especially after what happened in Detroit."

The dining room of The Phoenix was a large oval. Its linen-draped tables were busy with merchants conducting business over food, travelers eating alone, and one couple whose antics suggested they were recently wed.

Cabot and Valiantine ate salt-cured ham, roasted potatoes, crowder peas, boiled greens, and hard-boiled eggs. They shared a bottle of red wine and ate slowly, pausing between bites for conversation.

The lieutenant said, "I must be honest and say you've impressed me. You know this town, you have solid connections, and clearly you've earned the respect of many men. Chief Taylor, perhaps, excluded."

"I've had the Chief's respect for some things. Some disdain for others. I think in some way he is simply disappointed I left the department."

"I see. But you've renewed all these professional relationships. Don't you have family you want to see?"

Cabot watched the wine in his glass as he swirled it. "I have no family to visit. I grew up at the Masonic Widows and Orphans home."

"I'm sorry, Cabot, I didn't mean to . . ."

"No, that's fine. Really, when Yankee Bligh took me under his wing, that was the first time I had anything quite like a family. But he died seven years ago. I suppose doing the best job I can as a Treasury agent is my way of thanking him for all he taught me."

Valiantine cleared his throat. "How seriously do you consider this Confederate angle?" he asked.

"It's just a possibility so far, like everything else we've thought of," Cabot said. "We don't have enough hard evidence to give weight to one thing over another."

"That bandit, Awanai—he apparently is vicious enough to destroy any threat. But a Southern sympathizer? For some reason, it seems unlikely."

"Do you suppose there's a movement afoot unconnected to the Confederacy? Some other secessionist group?"

"An overthrow of the existing government? Or a conspiracy to build a separate country within the nation? Aaron Burr plotted to accomplish the latter. Some of his work took place along the Ohio River, too, if my memory is correct."

"It could be either type of conspiracy, based on the little we know."

The lieutenant sighed into his napkin. "I'm not sure we know enough even to call it a little, at this point."

"And you've no other notions about how much Carnavon and Awanai looked alike? According to the information we requested, Carnavon had no twin, nor a male sibling."

Valiantine tossed his napkin to the table in frustration. "Nothing."

The hotel concierge approached with an envelope. "Detective Cabot, I apologize for the interruption. A messenger arrived and said it was urgent."

With a nod, Cabot took the note. "No longer a detective,

Nick. You can call me Mister. This is my partner, Michael Valiantine. Nick Gardner has helped me with many cases." Nick patted Cabot's shoulder and left. The agent opened the note. "Your boss, Wellington. Wants to know what we've found."

The familiar furrow appeared on Valiantine's brow. He took the note from Cabot, perused it, then folded and slid it into his vest pocket. He made a sound of disgust.

Cabot dabbed his napkin to his lips. "What now?"

Valiantine scowled and stood. "I'm going to soak my feet. Then I'm going to bed. You?"

"A drink first, I think."

Valiantine nodded. Cabot watched him leave the dining room. Then the agent got up from the table and left the room. But he didn't go into the bar. Instead, he exited the building.

The two Aero-Marshals met again in the dining room for breakfast: fried eggs, smoked sausage, beaten biscuits with butter and sorghum, grits with red-eye gravy, and fried apples with a pot of black coffee. Valiantine paused in spearing together a piece of sausage and a flap of egg white. "That's the third time you've yawned over your food. Bad bed?"

"Late to bed. I visited a brothel last night."

Valiantine's face turned red and he began to choke on the food he'd just swallowed. A passing waiter whacked him solidly on the back until the lieutenant waved him off.

He was guzzling coffee to clear his throat when Cabot said, "Actually, I went to three."

Valiantine spewed coffee back into his cup. Tears ran from his eyes. "Good God, stop!"

Cabot waved a nonchalant gesture with his fork. "Oh, sorry, no, nothing of that nature. Purely professional interest. Bontonne supposed our quarry was retired from the military, and service men are known to visit such businesses. Indeed, if he wanted to remain hard to find, he may have taken up residence at one of the more reputable establishments."

Valiantine had gotten his breathing back to normal. After a last gasp, he asked, "What did you learn?"

"Not what I hoped, unfortunately. No customers in unfamiliar uniforms, or uniforms that had their insignia removed. But I learned that men with unusual accents had been paying for services the past two weeks."

"'Unusual accents'?" Valiantine drank more coffee. "The town is full of fresh immigrants. And boat crews from up and down the river are bound to pronounce words differently than the locals."

"The ladies are very familiar with just the things you mention. But the men they described had a distinctive accent, they said. And all the same sort of accent. One or two of the women asked these customers where they hailed from."

"And the answer?"

"Vague responses. One telling answer, however, that a wise-eyed lady remembered was 'the Northern Tier.'"

"That's not a description you hear often. New England, isn't it?"

"I think so. But I've never heard anyone say 'the Northern Tier' in a conversation as the place he calls home. Why not name a town or state?"

Valiantine nodded. "Sounds evasive. Odd." He frowned at his partner. "How did you know where to go?"

"You know I once worked for the police department. One learns much of life in that job. And, in the case of any new establishments, I simply read the newspaper advertisements—one must know the right phrases to look for."

"Hmmph. Why didn't you take me? Or at least tell me where you were going?"

"Sorry. I didn't know how you would take the suggestion."

"I'm a military man, Cabot, not a priest. And we agreed for each to keep the other informed."

While Valiantine spoke, Nick Gardner appeared again, bearing another note. Valiantine read this one. "Assistant Director Gallows this time. Wants to know what we've learned." The lieutenant tucked the paper into his breast pocket. "They're certainly anxious about our progress."

Now a waiter handed Cabot a folded note. After reading it, the agent looked up with an energized expression. "Mr. Bibb has news. River men reported seeing lights in the clouds over the river last night. And a fellow 'wearing a strange outfit' has been asking odd questions of wharf workers."

The two picked up their hats and started for the street. Valiantine asked, "Are we going to walk again?"

"It's not that far."

Just outside the front door of The Phoenix, a uniformed policeman dashed up to the pair. "Mr. Cabot! Chief Taylor has something for you to see."

"Headquarters?"

"No, Mr. Cabot. The mortuary."

Cabot's eyebrows rose. He turned to Valiantine. "Your feet are in luck. We'll need a cab."

Police Chief Taylor stood inside the door of the mortuary. He offered no greeting, only a scowl.

"The details you offered me suggested your investigation delves into the unusual," he said. "The evidence inside should meet those qualifications."

The Aero-Marshals followed Taylor along a hallway and down stairs. Through a black door, they entered a chilly room, brightly lit, with a slab at its center.

"Dear God."

Cabot didn't hear Valiantine's ejaculation. He was swallowed by a sense of drowning. All his senses focused on the body lying atop the slab. The head and limbs were torn from the torso, which was slashed deeply enough to expose the broken ribs and the mangled organs within. The parts had been arranged in their proper places on the slab, but the gaps between the pieces remained. The image brought to mind the fate Cabot had escaped in Kansas. His chest tightened against his ability to breathe.

He gulped a deep breath and gathered his wits before Taylor's scrutiny.

"Recognize him?" the chief asked.

Cabot answered, "No. Any information?"

"Found along the riverside by an old man collecting driftwood. Northeast of the wharf, just after dawn. Spread over an area about twenty square yards. The left foot, you'll notice, is missing. We think it's lost in the river."

While Taylor spoke, Cabot circled the corpse. He'd calmed his mind, evened his breathing, and was studying the body for clues.

"Birds and animals have been at him. How long dead?" Cabot asked.

Cabot and Valiantine had been so mesmerized by the corpse, they'd not noticed the man who now stepped forward from a corner of the room. He was bald, wore spectacles and a large rubberized bib apron decorated with a variety of stains. He smiled, and his bushy eyebrows twitched upward rapidly. The jumping eyebrows combined with the smile gave Cabot the sense the man was trying to help him understand some joke.

"The blood had drained out of the parts," the aproned man said. "From the body's condition, I'd say he was killed not last night, but the night before."

Cabot returned his gaze to the cadaver. "These slashes in the torso, on the limbs . . . they're very ragged. Perhaps made with a dull blade? Or claws?"

"No," the man said. "Neither, I think. Look, it's like someone with remarkably large hands tore into the flesh with his fingers. See? These could be four fingers, there a thumb. No sign of claw marks anywhere. But what sort of beast so large doesn't have claws? I'm at a loss, gentlemen, I'm sorry." The eyebrows twitched upward.

Cabot felt a momentary dizziness. He looked at the ravaged body laid out on the mortuary slab. He heard Yankee Bligh's voice: *The dead are graceless objects. They don't care about our desires for order and understanding. In return, we drop them here and flop them there as we need until they give up the answers we want.* He shook his head and looked around. "Was he wearing anything?"

"These," Taylor said. He pointed to a stack of fabric. It was dyed a very dark color, not quite black.

"We'll take those," Cabot said. "Can you wrap them in a parcel?"

"That's evidence!" Taylor thundered.

"Indeed, Chief Taylor," Valiantine said. "It may be evidence in our federal investigation as well. If not, the packet will be returned to your department."

Cabot realized he'd not looked at his partner since entering the room. He was thankful now the lieutenant had stepped up to interrupt Taylor, as Cabot didn't want to be the one to thwart his former superior officer. Cabot felt Taylor directed entirely too much enmity toward him already; he didn't care to feed Taylor's ill will further.

"May we see the spot the body was found?" Cabot asked.

"Yes," Taylor acceded. "Randall, the man who brought you here—he'll accompany you."

"We're done here," the agent said. "But, Chief Taylor, if it's possible . . . you might see if any of the professional ladies at Fanny Evans or Mary Edwards' establishments recognize the victim's face."

The man in the apron spoke up. "We'll make the head very presentable." His eyebrows twitched.

Outside the mortuary, the agents paused a few feet from the door. Cabot directed Randall to rouse the cab driver, who had dropped off to sleep, the reins in his hands.

Cabot saw a look of concern in Valiantine's face. "You're white as a sheet," the lieutenant said.

Cabot nodded. "You know the coin investigation in Kansas included murders. You didn't know the victims weren't simply killed. They were ripped to pieces."

"Damn."

"Yes. The coins, this body . . . this is our case, lieutenant."
Cabot handed over the brown-paper parcel. "Get another ride,
take this to Mr. Bibb. He can tell us, perhaps, what sort of
uniform it may be."

Valiantine nodded. "I'll have him stitch it together, show it to
Bontonne, see if he recognizes it."

"Good. And ask Richard for any news he's collected. He'll
trust you, since you met him with me."

"I'll meet you back at the hotel." Valiantine wrinkled his
nose. "I'll at least get away from this stench."

"About a mile thataway are the stockyards. We're at the edge
of the Butchertown neighborhood. Breakfast probably started its
way to our plates at the slaughterhouses a few blocks from here."

The lieutenant frowned and gestured at the mortuary.
"There's another butcher in town."

They separated, each to his tasks.

River Road paralleled the Ohio from the downtown wharf to
the northeast edge of the county. Away from the business bustle
huddled immediately around the wharf, few structures were
present along this lane used mainly by freighters.

About four miles from the wharf, Cabot pushed through the
fifty yards of tangled brush between the road and the river.
Randall pointed out the spots the cadaver's various parts had been
discovered. Cabot circled.

The edge of the tangle stood about ten feet above the level of
the river. A narrow game trail snaked along a couple of feet from
that edge. Cabot noted an eroded section where a second trail
veered off from the main track down the slope to a muddy shelf
leading into the current. Boot prints cluttered the slope path—
signs of the police who had recovered the body.

Other tracks crowded the shelf by the water. Cabot clambered
down, careful to stay out of the river. More boot prints. He
scoured eastward and found other tracks. The gait suggested they
were left by the man who had found the remains.

The agent continued along the shelf, whose width changed with the vagaries of the river.

He spotted a sign that drove a spike of cold between his shoulder blades. It matched the size and shape of the unusual prints he'd found in Kansas, where he'd discovered Mrs. Smith in a tree.

He slowed his breathing and took a closer look. The heel was partially washed away by the water. The toes pointed toward the bank, only about eight feet high here. Part of another print remained on the slope itself, pointing upward.

Cabot climbed up to the edge, back into the thick brush. He found no more signs he could recognize. Roughly a hundred yards farther to the east started a dense thicket.

The agent made his way to the road and waved Randall over to join him.

"Find anything?" Randall asked.

Instead of answering, Cabot pointed toward the woods. "What's in there?"

"Not much. Some river rats keep shacks in there. You know the type: like to be left to themselves, maybe they're a little crazy."

Cabot nodded. He looked at the sky over the river. "Any rain last night? Night before?"

Randall looked puzzled. "No, not a drop. Bit of a drought this month."

Cabot smiled at him. "No, you're right. Not a cloud in the sky."

In the bar of The Phoenix, Cabot and Valiantine sat at a corner table away from other customers and ate cold cuts of meat and cheese with hard-boiled eggs and coffee. Randall stood near, wearing an expression of discomfort.

The lieutenant waved him to the lunch spread. "Help yourself."

While the policeman was occupied, Cabot gave his report. Valiantine followed: "Richard Bibb said men saw lights in clouds over the Ohio the night before we arrived."

"The stranger was killed that night," Cabot said.

"Yes. But other than the clouds over the river, the night was clear. Then, last night, more clouds and lights—and noises, banging and yelling. A couple of half-drunk fishermen heard this racket overhead. Said their boat was nearly overturned by a large splash near them."

"What?"

"Under the clouds and lights and furious yelling." Cabot watched a smile play with Valiantine's mouth. "More splashing, which the befuddled fools thought headed toward the Kentucky shore."

"Someone escaped the airship!"

"Someone or some*thing*." Valiantine's eyes narrowed. "No ghost—from Corn Island or anywhere else—destroyed that man on the mortuary slab."

Cabot's scalp tingled. "What else?"

"Bibb quick-stitched the uniform together. I showed it to Bontonne, and he said it matched the one worn by the fellow with the coins."

"Bontonne needs to see the dead man's face, see if it's the coin man. Where's Randall?" Cabot shook his head. "We're getting a lot of clues. But I've yet to figure what they mean."

Nick Gardner arrived bearing another note. Cabot scanned it. Valiantine stood to look for Randall while he spoke: "One last thing: Bibb couldn't identify the uniform's fabric. Not wool, cotton, linen, or any sort of blend. He's never seen its like."

Cabot scowled at the note. "That's odd. Richard is a remarkable expert in cloth identification. Say, do you know 'Executive Officer Barnaby Scarborough'?"

The lieutenant shook his head.

"Apparently he is a peer of Gallows and Wellington." Cabot looked up at Valiantine. "He, too, wants to know what we've learned."

"What's raised their interest beyond waiting for our usual reports?" Valiantine turned as Randall dashed into the room and stopped at their table. "What is it, man?"

Randall caught his breath. "They've found more body parts, sirs."

"Parts." Cabot stood. "I thought only a foot was missing from this morning's corpse."

Randall's eyes widened. "More parts, sir. Another victim."

The body had been found near the Portland Canal. Actually, only a leg had been found. A night guard on his way home from the lock house at dawn stepped on the limb where it lay on the levee path near the spot the coins had reportedly been found.

A forearm and the head were located in the brambles on the land side of the levee.

Cabot stood on the path looking down into the brush. "Any clues on the path have been trampled out by your companions from the department," he said to Randall. He pointed at the tangle. "But you can see broken shrub and tree limbs in a crooked line from the levee over to the road on the Portland side. Something big tore through to get to the clear space. Probably to escape from the murder site."

Randall had kept his left fist over his mouth since he'd seen the victim's remains. "Why would he run through that thicket? The path up here is clear. Easier going."

"Good question." Cabot turned to look at the river. "Maybe there was something or someone over here"—his eyes scanned the clear sky—"the killer wanted to get away from."

Valiantine approached. He'd been questioning the bleary-eyed watchman who'd found the leg. Cabot saw the now-familiar furrow on his partner's brow.

"Didn't hear, didn't see anything," the lieutenant said.

"The blood was still sticky," Cabot said. "It couldn't have happened too long before he found the evidence."

"Over here!"

A policeman waved from the waterside, thirty yards east of their position. The trio scrambled down the slope to join him.

He stood in the edge of the water. By one booted foot, a partially submerged arm rocked in the current.

Valiantine retrieved the limb. "Two arms. We'll soon have half a body."

Cabot noticed a fresh expression of distress taking over Randall's features.

Valiantine voiced an oath. "The sleeve is dry. It's been in the water, but it just drained from the cloth like through a sieve. Completely dry, not even damp."

Cabot examined the ripped fabric. "Mr. Bibb will need to see this."

Another shout, fifty yards west toward the lock house: "Here! Here!"

Another policeman had waded into the current to snag a body part he'd spotted bobbing in the water. Cabot helped him onto dry land as Valiantine took the recovered limb.

Cabot saw a new look of perplexity on his partner's face.

"It's a third arm."

"You're telling me a monster is running loose in my city!"

Police Chief Taylor's words still rang in Cabot's ears just as they had two hours ago.

Monster. Cabot had avoided using the word. But now Taylor had said it aloud, and it sat more easily in the agent's thoughts. But *easy* didn't mean Cabot was comfortable with the notion of the thing at large, able to rend a human being to lifeless tatters.

They'd recovered parts of three bodies, but only one head. Like the first head, it would be used for possible identification, but Cabot didn't hope for much.

Richard Bibb had been unable to identify the second fabric type, although, he'd said, it differed from that of the first uniform. Enough scraps had been pulled from the batch of partial cadavers to assemble a suit with a military cut, but it looked very different from the first uniform. Even the color differed—pale gray instead of nearly black.

Again, the look matched the cut of no known military uniform.

Bibb ran a scrap of the cloth through his fingers. "This is very remarkable stuff. Yes, different from the other fabric you brought me."

After leaving Richard's workshop, Cabot asked Valiantine, "Does this mean we are dealing with two differing groups? Two . . . armies or militias?"

The lieutenant sighed, a worried sound. "It is starting to look that way."

A bloodhound had been put on the trail from the levee path. It worked its way through Portland alleys and backyards. Homeowners reported their dogs, horses, and chickens being disturbed during the morning hours.

The hound led them east into Louisville, near the wharf, then along out-of-the-way paths away from the business district.

Eventually the Aero-Marshals stood by Randall near River Road looking at the thicket Cabot had faced that morning. The lieutenant asked, "How far does this extend?"

Randall shrugged. "Miles. And a ways along, it spreads to both sides of the road. Big patches of swamp in there, too."

By the edge of the timber, the hound heaved against its handler's leash.

Cabot said, "The woods are thick enough that we'll be at a disadvantage. Randall, tell Chief Taylor we need more men—at least twenty. With guns."

"Ten gauge shotguns, if you've got them," Valiantine said. "Loaded with buckshot or solid slugs."

Randall's eyes widened. He nodded, and then tramped away.

Valiantine scowled at the sky. "I don't want to be in that tangle after dark with that thing."

"No," Cabot said. "No, you don't."

"We will form an L," Valiantine directed. "From the top of the slope bordering the river along the front edge of the timber, then up alongside the road. When the woods spread to the other side of the road, the wing of the L will swing across the road, and we'll have one straight line advancing through the trees. I'll be at the hinge of the L."

"I'll be at the head of the L, by the river," Cabot said.

The lieutenant surveyed the men arrayed before him. "Everyone armed? Take your places."

The line of men advanced. The bloodhound put its nose to the ground and pulled its handler forward. Cabot and Valiantine each carried a shotgun brought by the Police Department.

The thick growth of trees and briars impeded their forward progress. The tangles of limbs clutched at the men's clothes, scratched at their faces and eyes, and slowed their advance so that the searchers were sweaty and weary after only an hour.

BANG!

A gunshot halted the advance. The men dropped to their knees or dodged behind the bole of a tree, guns at the ready.

Valiantine bellowed out, "Who's shooting?"

A reedy voice replied: "Me, you sunnavabitch! You got my dog but you ain't gettin' me!"

The lieutenant muttered a curse. "We're the police. We don't know anything about your dog. We're armed, and we outnumber you. We'll shoot you down if you fire again. We're coming forward."

He paused a moment for a reply. Hearing nothing, Valiantine nodded, and the line of men advanced.

They reached a shack assembled like a crazy quilt of driftwood, scraps of corrugated metal, broken boards from shipping crates. A scrawny terrier of a man with an unkempt beard stood with a Spencer carbine in his hands. He challenged them: "I ain't done nothin' to you. Leave me alone!"

Cabot had come up from his end of the line. "We're looking for a murderer."

"A monster," Valiantine interjected.

"I saw somethin'," the hermit said. "Size of a bear. Did that to my dog." Tears came to his eyes when he gestured at a carcass lying twenty feet away: a large dog, its body ripped in two.

"I'm sorry," Cabot said. "We're not here to bother you. We'll keep on our way. But if you see the thing again, shoot to kill. Or hide."

The man glowered from within the nest of hair that hid most of his face. The police line moved forward again. Before departing back to his place in the line, Cabot spoke to his partner: "We've been at this more than an hour. It'll start getting dark soon."

"Every third man has a lantern."

Cabot's breathing felt too shallow to fill his chest. "We don't want to meet this thing after dark. And the danger of the men shooting their fellows if we do—"

"We must stop this thing."

Cabot looked at his partner. He nodded, and returned to his place at the head of the line.

The sun had dropped below the horizon, and the light was fading from the sky. Cabot paused and surveyed the river. He saw a mass of clouds building at the crests of the Indiana hills across the river to the northwest. Rain would make the search truly impossible.

The agent tromped onward, pushing through waist-high brush and past gnarled, scrubby trees twice his height. He still could see the man to his right, a few yards off. Soon he would be a featureless figure visible only because he moved among the motionless shapes of the thicket, and his presence would be known only by the sounds he made in the darkness.

The dusk was nearly complete. The nighttime breeze was picking up from the river. Cabot glanced in that direction. The cloud formation was very large now, and had detached from the silhouette of the Indiana hills to drift to the east. Cabot prepared to shout out to call off the search, but stopped to watch the cloud.

It was a dark mass, darker than the twilight-thickening sky. It moved faster than the breeze Cabot felt on his face, but he supposed the wind might move more quickly at a higher elevation.

And then he saw the lights: a there-and-gone glimmer of pinpoints shining from within the cloud itself.

Cabot stood mesmerized a moment. He noticed he had

unconsciously raised the shotgun to his shoulder and pointed it toward the cloud. He raised his voice: "Valiantine!"

And then he heard shouts behind him.

He turned. Many yards away the hound began to bay in a strangled fashion, followed by a strange, canine squeal that suddenly cut off. A human scream. The *boom* of firing shotguns. He heard Valiantine yelling orders.

Cabot heard the crash of plants ripping and breaking as something charged through the thicket.

Toward his position.

Cabot felt a rising tide of panic flood his chest. He glanced at the cloud, the outlines of which were melting into the greater darkness of the sky; he turned and faced the oncoming threat.

He aimed the shotgun toward the source of the approaching noises.

"Stop!" he shouted.

The crashing came closer. Rapidly.

"Halt!" he yelled, louder.

The crashing grew louder.

Thirty feet away.

Twenty feet.

Ten.

Cabot fired.

The half second after he pulled the trigger, Cabot heard a tremendous bellow. A hurtling weight smashed into him. He lost his grip on the gun and cart-wheeled through space.

The agent splashed into the river. He thrashed his way to the surface and gulped for air.

A bolt of light cut the dark from the body of the cloud overhead to the river's rushing surface. Thunder boomed and bright flashes lit the interior of the cloud. Geysers of water shot up from the river.

Cabot wasted no breath on swearing, but kicked at the water and helped the current take him westward away from the immediate violence. After the *booms* he heard shouts, followed by more booming.

At some point he grew aware he lay on the muddy shelf of the river bank. His feet and legs remained in the water, and the river tugged at his limbs. He drew up his legs. He'd lost a shoe.

Cabot hadn't even been conscious of clawing his way to shore. He sucked down deep, rattling breaths. The booming had ceased. He heard no more shouts.

The agent wasn't sure where he'd come ashore. Somewhere between the ruckus and the wharf, he guessed. Once the trembling in his limbs stopped, after he'd regained some composure and a bit of energy, he would stand, climb the slope, and determine his whereabouts.

Right now, he concentrated on simply breathing.

And while his breathing settled, he focused on the image burned into his mind: the beam of light from the cloud that had illuminated the beast in the water, the monster he had shot, the thing that had knocked him into the water—the momentary flash of a child's frightened face.

ABOVE IT ALL

Jim Beard

September 1897

Chagrinned at a miniscule spot of some unidentifiable matter that defied his covert attempt at removing it from his coat with a fingernail, Lieutenant Michael Valiantine sighed and turned his gaze to the denuded cherry trees outside the window. The sight of them only served to depress him more.

Major Wellington looked up from his reading of the lieutenant's report, apparently jostled from it by the sigh. Frowning slightly, the major returned to his perusal of the papers. Valiantine looked at Agent Cabot, who sat next to him in front of Wellington's desk.

He's not in a good state, Valiantine thought to himself, observing his partner. *Hasn't mentioned his Yankee Bligh all day.*

Valiantine figured the man's funk stemmed from the events in Kentucky and whatever it was Cabot saw there in the river. From then on, the younger agent had been reluctant to discuss it, no matter that Valiantine urged him to do so. The lieutenant made up his mind to not press him, that he'd soon enough care to talk. Or not.

"Ridiculous."

He looked back to the major to find his superior's eyes upon him.

"Beg pardon, sir?"

Wellington glared at the lieutenant, weaving his fingers together and pressing them down upon the report he'd let fall to his desktop. Valiantine steeled himself for an outburst, though he couldn't reason why one should come if it did.

"This report, Lieutenant," Wellington said. "Proud of it are you?"

The two agents had written the report together, more or less, and had held almost nothing back, even Cabot's thoughts on the final moments of their latest case. Valiantine thought it would be somewhat eye-opening to the major and his fellow bureaucrats who had dogged them with demands for information throughout their trip to Kentucky. What it all exactly meant, though, was still murky. If anything, the lieutenant believed it to show progress in his and Cabot's investigations of the airships.

He told the major just that, and with a clear conscience.

"Nonsense," the man replied. "More than nonsense, actually. This report is utter fantasy."

Valiantine's face grew warm and he found himself unable to speak; this wasn't what he expected. He'd assumed there'd be some small resistance to what they'd uncovered, but his superior's outright denial of the report set him on unstable ground.

"I say again, Lieutenant," Wellington continued, "are you proud of this and your other reports? Proud to be wasting my time in this fashion? Wasting the government's time and money?"

Valiantine began to find his voice, but was silenced when the major suddenly slammed a fist down on his desk, disturbing a nearby ink bottle.

"Damn you, be quiet," he growled. "Don't speak. You were sent out to look into a matter of possible great importance to this country and you've done nothing to this point but flit here and there, looking up at the sky and writing reports about clouds and vapors. Valiantine, I expected better of you, honestly."

The lieutenant's breath caught at the rebuke, but before he could muster any return fire, his partner waded into the fray.

"Apologies, *sir*," Cabot seethed, sitting forward in his chair, "but I can't understand you. We've done everything that—"

Wellington tore his gaze from Valiantine to skewer the Treasury man with it.

"Hold your tongue, Cabot. I will not have you speaking to me in that tone here in my own damned office."

The younger man stood up, his swift gesture knocking his chair back on its rear legs. In a split second of starling clarity, Valiantine saw what was to come next.

"I question your authority over me," Cabot said in a calm voice. He turned away from the major's desk and moved toward the office's door to the corridor outside.

Wellington thumped his desk again with his fist, but did not rise from his chair. Instead, he sat back, almost casually, and stared at the departing agent.

"Doesn't matter, Cabot," he said with some smugness, bringing the Treasury man to an abrupt halt. "You're mistaken in your opinion, but it doesn't matter. You and Valiantine here are being put on ice."

Both agents turned to fix Wellington with questioning looks, then each other.

"What do you mean?" Valiantine asked his superior.

The major smiled grimly, looking back to his desk and clearing away the report he'd discarded.

"You're both suspended from duty," he told the duo without looking up at them. "Temporarily, until I confer with others as to the worth and future of the investigation. Until then, Department A-13 doesn't exist anymore until I say otherwise.

"Dismissed."

Cabot found the lieutenant three days later, at the Smithsonian Institution, deep among the bric-a-brac displayed throughout its halls.

Looking up with mild interest at his partner, who stood there hat in hand and somber, Valiantine sighed and raised an eyebrow, as if to bid the man to speak.

"Thought I'd find you here, or someplace similar," Cabot told him. "You seem like the sort that—"

The lieutenant turned his back to him, cutting him off with a dismissive wave of his hand.

"You don't know a damn thing about what I seem or not seem, sir."

Cabot did not speak again for a minute or so. He stood there silently, staring at Valiantine until he turned to reflect upon the object of the man's scrutiny, a glass-walled display case. In it sat a dark, lumpy stone. A small card lay next to the stone.

"We have a new report." Though he did not speak loudly, his voice echoed a bit in the hall in which they stood.

"And we are on suspension, Cabot. Hasn't that sunk in yet after three whole days?"

The younger man continued, undeterred. "Luray, Virginia. Near Massanutten Mountain, roughly sixty, seventy miles from here. They've been seeing lights there."

The lieutenant digested that, his back still to Cabot. "And how is it we have this report, seeing as there is no longer a Department A-13?"

The Treasury man smiled slightly. "Someone, perhaps a junior agent, did not receive word of that, apparently. The report arrived upon my desk this morning. I didn't question it."

"And these lights?" Valiantine asked, turning toward Cabot.

"At night, up on the mountain. Townspeople say they don't see them every night, but frequently, and when they do there are odd sounds that accompany them. One man reported he'd heard . . . a band playing."

The lieutenant swung around fully, staring with great interest at his partner.

"Thought that would do it," Cabot said simply.

"We'd be disobeying direct orders," Valiantine said.

"Indeed. When do we begin?"

"Immediately, if we're in complete agreement."

"I believe there's a line that will take us directly into Luray."

"No," Valiantine said, holding up a hand. "We'd be too exposed, too many ways to track us, once they realize we're gone. Besides, I'm sick of trains."

Cabot fingered his hat, letting out a breath. "A coach, then. But it will be more than a day before we'd reach the spot. Possibly closer to two."

"That doesn't worry me," the lieutenant said, his eyes on something intangible in the distance. "Citizens of this country have died. Something is very wrong. We are being threatened from the outside. We must continue to act, no matter the cost."

Finally, he focused on Cabot again. "Can you make the arrangements? And quietly?"

The Treasury man turned on his heel, heading for the exit. "I know how to be circumspect," he threw over his shoulder.

"Cabot? Perhaps we need to take the time to analyze this further?"

Cabot paused, but did not look back. "We have at least an entire day of a bumpy, dirty coach ride ahead of us to chitchat," he said. "Don't forget that."

Valiantine smiled, nodding. He turned to take in the display case once more, his eyes memorizing every nook and cranny of the meteorite that lay within.

While they rode along on the journey, past the borders of Washington, D.C. and into the surrounding countryside, the lieutenant could not tear his gaze from the mountains ahead of them. He'd been all over the world and had seen many a range, but as they approached Massanutten and the Shenandoah line beyond it, he fought the urge to see them as ominous harbingers of what was to come.

As it turned out, they talked very little over the almost two full days it took them to reach the little town in Virginia, nestled between the hills and mountains of Appalachia. Thankfully, they had the coach to themselves, though its driver made more than one remark over the long hours as to why "two fine gentlemen would want to ride the roads when a perfectly good railroad was to be had."

Upon their arrival, Valiantine paid the man above and beyond the proscribed fare and thanked him for his service and for his discretion. The driver smiled broadly as he accepted the money.

Things couldn't get much stranger, could they? the Army man asked himself, wondering if Cabot was also caught in the grip of dark, inner forces. Interestingly, the younger man seemed to brighten a bit from the trip, perhaps putting the incident in Kentucky behind him, or at least in reserve until such time as to examine it further.

They found the town of Luray to be as small and as quiet as they'd imagined. Arriving late in the day, Valiantine peered all around as they exited the coach, trying to ascertain Luray's geography as night fell about them. In all, it appeared to be no different than thousands of other such towns that dotted the American landscape, save for its point of interest to their mission.

The dirt street they stood upon fell away to the north and south in slight tiers or steppes, the buildings around them simple wooden structures, worn but otherwise in good repair. To the east, mountains loomed in the distance, as well as to the west, which Valiantine knew to be the Massanutten. Few people walked the streets of Luray at that time of day, but he didn't think it strange.

Cabot spotted an inn a few doors away from the telegraph office in front of which they paused, standing in the street with their bags in hand. They made their way to the establishment, checked in with a story of wanting to do a bit of climbing and bird-watching, and found the inn offered libations as well as meals. Shortly thereafter, the two agents leaned against a bar in one corner of the inn's dining room and listened to a most amazing story related by the innkeeper himself, a man who introduced himself as Mr. Bamen.

"Go on," Valiantine urged, taking another small sip of his

beer. He disliked the stuff, normally, but found that by nursing a mug of it he won more confidences than mistrust.

"Well," Bamen continued, his blonde slicked-back hair gleaming and long nose twitching, "these fairy lights come and go, come and go."

Cabot had finished his own beer and ordered another; Valiantine approved of his tactics. "You say people also heard music? Surely that's not unusual with other people around?"

Bamen chortled low in his throat. "It is if there ain't no band about, sir, meanin' no disrespect. We haven't had a band in this town in decades, and we ain't never had no orchestra. The constable himself heard the music, plain as day. I ain't about to question his sanity. And he saw the lights, too."

"Must be a lot of stories like that in this part of the country, eh?" Valiantine asked casually. "Legends, tales, that sort of thing." He tried to sound indifferent about it.

"Sure," Bamen said, "we have all of 'em, certainly. The black dogs and the wise babies and the frogs fallin' out of the skies . . . even the big hairy men and the little wee ones, too. But I ain't never heard much before about lights like giant eyes up on Massanutten accompanied by highfalutin' music. No, sir, that's downright strange."

The lieutenant almost laughed at what the man considered "strange," considering the laundry list of odd subjects he'd just rattled off. Instead, he looked Bamen straight in the eye and pointed a finger at him.

"What do you think of it all, Mr. Bamen? If you had to speculate; what would you say it all amounts to?"

The innkeeper paused in his wiping away at the bar top, obviously pondering the question. Finally, he spoke.

"I don't like it, if I'm to be truthful about it. One queer thing, maybe that's all it is. Two? Perhaps there's a bit more to it. But when you have ghost lights on the mountain and phantom music and strangers passing through and the young man who got all bit up, well—"

Cabot's hand shot out and clamped down on Bamen's wrist. The man looked up at the Treasury agent, his eyes wide and his brow furrowed in confusion.

"Bit up? When? Where?"

"Three days ago," the innkeeper said in a strangled voice. "Young feller from just outside of Luray. Bear got 'im. Mauled him something fierce. He lived, thank the Good Lord . . ."

Valiantine had set his mug down, unsure of whether or not to tell Cabot to release the man's arm. "Where, Mr. Bamen?"

"Up on the mountain," Bamen said, quietly, slowly, as if piecing something together. "But . . . it was a bear, I tell you!"

But he was addressing thin air. His two customers had moved to a table on the far side of the room and were deep in conversation.

"When?" Cabot asked, his face grim.

"Crack of dawn," Valiantine replied. "But we may need some equipment. At the very least some better footwear. Heavier coats for both of us would also be nice; it will likely be cold up there, this time of year."

His partner nodded. "He said 'strangers passing through,' also. Should we assume that there are two factions involved?"

"Dammit," Valiantine said. "We're making leaps in logic like March hares. But what else are we to do? We must assume that we're in the middle of something and that we're in danger of giving away our position at any given time. We're alone in this now, Cabot; we have virtually no resources to fall back upon should things get dicey."

"Did we ever?"

The lieutenant appraised the younger man's question, nodding. "Unknown. So much is unknown. Let's get a good night's sleep and attack this full on in the morning."

As it turned out, with constant thoughts about Mr. Bamen's story, Valiantine didn't sleep much at all.

The next morning the two agents sought out the general store in Luray and were pleased to find that it stocked proper boots and coats for climbing, as well as a few other provisions for their trek up Massanutten.

They also discovered the store's proprietor had seen the lights on the mountain, too, and pointed them toward its northern section. Valiantine thanked the man with a friendly-yet-blasé tone and paused only briefly while exiting when the man urged Cabot and him to "mind the bears and rattlers."

Scouting the base of Massanutten in the first rays of morning sun, they came upon what seemed to be an old trail, which began behind an ancient, immense tulip tree.

"Up the airy mountain, eh?" Valiantine said, looking at the mountainside.

"I'd rather the rushy glen," Cabot replied, pulling his hat down tight.

Shortly into their ascent they decided their decision to forego actual mountain climbing gear such as spikes and ropes and the like was an accurate one; Massanutten was not steep, though it was not a walk in the park on a Sunday afternoon, either. Valiantine had scaled mountains as far off as Nicaragua, while Cabot's experiences in more arduous forms of field work were not as extensive as his partner's. Still, he did not complain and kept up with the army man.

The Treasury man offered a suggestion early in the climb: to give themselves time to observe their surroundings and catalog it for future reference. This he supported by another of his Yankee Bligh *bon mots*, one which Valiantine realized was sound and logical. They'd be away from civilization while on the mountain and, depending upon what they'd encounter there, likely to have to move about it in less than optimal conditions, meaning, in the dark, under fire, chased by wild animals, or any of a dozen or so other extreme situations.

They met with wild turkey, deer, and definite signs of bear. The trail they'd accessed was sparse at points, wholly disappearing into wildflowers and other flora at others. Valiantine had never fully grasped the intricacies of trailblazing and tracking, so he trusted his instincts and Cabot's keen eyes to keep their feet on solid ground and moving ever upward.

By dusk, the two men had gained a height of almost two-thousand feet, more than two-thirds of Massanutten's full elevation. They'd also seen the track of some large animal of which neither of them could wholly identify.

"Why music?" Cabot asked as they rested for a moment on a shelf of sandstone, near a grove of trees. Branches from a dead oak lay all about them.

Valiantine took his meaning immediately. "It does seem incongruous, doesn't it? Hallucinations by the witnesses? Interpreting something else as music they recognize?"

Cabot chewed on that one for a few seconds. "Those vapors we discovered at Carnavon's compound play some important role in all this. I feel fairly certain of it."

"Absolutely," Valiantine said, looking up at their destination again, the mountaintop, as it faded into the night. "I'm thinking along those same lines. What if—"

A bestial howl split the somber atmosphere of the mountain-side. Both men's hands flew to their coatpockets, fingering the revolvers within.

"Coyote?" Cabot asked.

"No, I don't believe so."

"I'm guessing that's not a deer or a snake, then."

"If it is," Valiantine whispered, "then we are in for a bit of trouble."

As it turned out, they were in for quite a bit of trouble.

Valiantine, pistol in hand, waved at Cabot. "Down, down; present as small a target as possible." He himself lowered his center of gravity and extended one knee to the ground, looking all about him, urging his eyes to acclimate to the darkness.

A huge, black figure rose up not thirty feet from them, from behind a gigantic fallen tree they'd passed on the way up, and sprinted lightning-fast past them, passing within only five feet or so of their position.

Valiantine tracked the thing with his pistol, finger tensing on its trigger.

"No, wait!" Cabot said, grasping at his partner's hand. "Don't fire!"

A resounding, guttural growl filled their ears as the dark shape gained a spot on the other side of them, between two trees. It stopped there, and both men could see that it swung around to face them.

"Are you mad, Cabot? If that's the . . . if it's . . . I won't sit here and—"

The thing flung itself abruptly from its hiding spot, running directly toward them, howling, arms extended in front of it.

Valiantine fired. The thing flinched from the bullet's impact on its shoulder, but kept moving.

The lieutenant took an instinctual step backwards, his foot slipping on the loose rock shelving behind him. A drop-off. They were near a drop-off. But how far down did it go?

Cabot discharged his own pistol. The thing's left arm flew up in a strange way. It howled in pain, but did not slow in its headlong sprint toward them.

Valiantine grabbed at a large, forked branch that lay on the rock next to him. The very second he set its one end into the ground by his feet, pointing its fork upward, the great, dark figure was upon him.

Catching it with the branch, he put all his strength into taking the impact of the flying body. A loud crack like a gunshot told him the branch snapped under the pressure, but he tried to use his assailant's momentum to drive it past him.

The figure flew over his head, a huge black monstrosity. Something caught at his scalp and he felt a sharp pain there.

Howling like an Irish banshee, the creature toppled past the rock shelf and down into even deeper darkness below it.

Huffing and puffing, Valiantine finally came to rest on solid ground many yards from his starting point. Fear had propelled him from the site of the attack, but it had subsided and he felt he could stop running with some modicum of safety.

He was not ashamed of allowing fear overtake him; he knew well that it had saved his life on other occasions and when to allow it free rein.

Breathing somewhat more regularly, he looked around and found himself immersed in almost total darkness. He tasted something salty on his lips, felt a warm, wet sensation on his scalp and forehead, and knew he was bleeding. This was confirmed when he reached up and probed the wound on his head; it was long and fairly deep, slick with blood.

The lieutenant let out a sigh, his fingers trembling slightly. A jolt of panic coursed through him, but he fought it back and tried to discern his surroundings, realizing with a start that he was alone.

"Cabot!" It came out of him with more volume than he intended. When he received no reply, he began to grow angry. "Cabot, dammit; where are you?"

"Here . . ."

The voice of his partner came from somewhere nearby, and from a slightly higher elevation than that which he currently occupied. He started to move toward it, pushing aside thick vegetation and colliding with tree trunks. Finally, he saw night sky and stars.

The silhouette of Cabot stood out against the sky; Valiantine could tell his partner was looking back over his shoulder at him, but also pointing to something he did not immediately see at first.

"There," the Treasury man said, calmly, as if pointing out another wild turkey or a peculiarly colored gentian.

Valiantine followed the line of Cabot's index finger up and toward the mountain. He saw the light his partner indicated.

Valiantine reached Cabot and they stood shoulder to shoulder, gazing at it, a mildly bright orb of illumination that seemed to bounce a bit in the air, not unlike a child's balloon on string, buffeted by a spring breeze.

"I'm sorry I could not shoot at first," Cabot said. "But after what I saw in Kentucky . . ."

"Forget it," Valiantine said. "Damn thing got me good, though."

He sensed that Cabot turned toward him in the darkness. "Bad?"

"No," the lieutenant replied, "I said 'good.' It struck me a winning blow. I'm bleeding. Badly."

"Then let's—"

Valiantine cut him off by placing one hand on the man's arm and turning him to look back at the light, or the absence thereof. It had gone out.

In its place stood a structure, a high tower of a sort.

"No sounds," Cabot said. Valiantine thought he was urging him to be quiet, but realized his partner meant to point out the complete absence of noise in the area. They were encased in a zone of absolute silence: no birds, no insects, nothing.

All at once, a light blinked on in the sky to the south of their position, drawing their attention from the tower. There was no way to discern the distance or size of it, but the light did not falter, merely glowed steadily.

Suddenly, the new light began to blink on and off. From their vantage point, the two agents could see the tower and the light in the sky were related, and the latter seemed to be trying to signal to the former.

"Code?" the lieutenant asked, in awe of the spectacle despite himself.

Cabot wagged his head. "None that I know of. Not Morse, though there is . . ."

The tower light returned, a quick burst that disappeared as quickly as it came. A heartbeat or two later, the other light went away. Darkness prevailed again.

"Let's get in closer to that tower." Valiantine pointed to their right, and Cabot seemed to take his meaning: skirt the small clearing in front of the structure and stay to the tree line.

With wary glances skyward, they inched closer to the base of the tower.

"That was answer and response," Cabot noted. Valiantine grunted his agreement.

When they got within twenty feet of the tower, they observed the structure. Constructed of stone block and immense lengths of wood, Valiantine had never seen anything quite like it. He could not fathom how it could have been built so far up the mountainside, though he admired its stout look and obvious structural integrity. Past that, its architectural style defied his categorization. It appeared wholly alien to him, though he'd been around the world and seen much in his career.

From its extensive weathering and cracking, they found the tower's base to be older than the rest of the structure, guessing it to be at least thirty years old or more. Cabot opined that it may have been built during the war, or shortly before it.

The Treasury man also pointed out the dome that sat at the top of the tower, some one hundred feet above the structure's base. It looked to be made entirely of metal, with gigantic seams running from its top, central point to its circumference.

"Good Lord," Valiantine whispered, "is that an observatory?"

They sat in silence for several minutes, assessing the scene, and watching the night sky for the return of the light. Either something had been approaching the tower and completed its flight in total darkness, or it still hung in space at some unknown distance from the structure, waiting for who knew what.

"We need to get in there," Valiantine said, nodding. "This may be the key to it all."

The two men continued their trek along the tree line and carefully approached the tower's base. Touching it, feeling along the length of its stone construction, Valiantine felt justified in his guess at its age; it was clear that the tower was built atop the foundation of an older structure. Though it appeared strange in its design, its materials did not show the extensive age of its base.

"If we find there's someone inside this," Cabot began, pointing at what looked to be a doorway set into the base, "we must assume they may be joined by others." The younger man tipped his chin upward to indicate the night sky to the south.

"Agreed," Valiantine said. Finding a wide metal door with a handle, he pulled on it and found it unlocked.

With Cabot right behind him, they entered the tower.

Five sets of eyes turned their way. Valiantine could see they were not expected.

The interior of the tower was lit, but by what means was not immediately evident. The air was hazy, even murky; it felt very familiar to the lieutenant. The room they'd entered was fairly large, a square that seemed to occupy the entire base of the structure, with a high ceiling that he wanted to observe, but didn't dare take his eyes from the tower's inhabitants.

There were four men and a woman. Each of them wore a one-piece garment that covered them from neck to toe, a comfortable looking arrangement with no clear buttons or fasteners. Valiantine thought the fabric looked something like what they'd found in Kentucky, or one of the samples, at least. The men wore their hair short, cropped close to the scalp; the woman sported a short bob.

One of the men stepped toward the agents. When he did, Valiantine caught sight of a corner of the immaculately clean room that was strewn with straw and featured a large, heavy chain bolted by one end to the wall.

The room was silent save for the soft strains of a symphony that he didn't immediately recognize. This too, like the illumination and the haze, presented no clear source.

"I . . . I don't understand . . ." the man said, stopping roughly ten feet from the agents. "How did you get up here?"

Valiantine produced his pistol, pointed it at the man. Out of the corner of the eye he saw Cabot did likewise.

"Who are you?" he demanded. "Please identify yourselves."

The man hesitated. Valiantine caught a quick, minute glance upward. Risking it, he turned his own eyes to the ceiling of the room and discovered there wasn't one. Above them, the walls of the tower stretched up to what seemed to be the metal dome they saw from the outside, but he couldn't be sure, for the damnable haze was thicker in the space. He also saw what looked to be stairs that wound around the inside of the tower.

Movement drew his eyes back to the group in front of him. The woman had stepped forward and past the man.

"You cannot be here," she said in a honeyed voice, yet with no accompanying smile.

"We are Federal agents," Cabot said, holding up his badge with one hand, his pistol never wavering from the group. "This is all very peculiar."

Valiantine's head swam and the scene before him lurched suddenly. He resisted an urge to reach up and touch the dried blood on his forehead, to wipe it away and rearrange himself. *What a fright I must look*, he thought to himself. *Stay awake, Michael!*

He took a step toward the woman, his pistol pointed at her midsection. She was very handsome, her appealing figure straining at her coveralls in an almost obscene manner. Valiantine, maddened by the unbidden observation, shoved it aside and raised his pistol higher.

"You are under arrest, all of you," he told the group, squeezing the grip of his weapon until it bit into his hand. "We must determine the purpose of this operation."

"On what charge?" the woman asked.

Behind her, one of the men moved to the wall closest to Valiantine and reached out to grasp at a large flywheel set there.

Someone discharged a pistol. There was a flash and the explosive sound and the man was flung backward, blood fountaining from his shoulder.

Valiantine saw a small puff of smoke arise from his weapon and realized it was he who had fired.

All at once, the woman was on him, clawing at his coat, wrestling with him for the pistol.

The room spun like a carousel. Someone grabbed him from behind. An arm tightened around his throat as he pulled at it, trying to release the pressure on his windpipe. He thought he heard Cabot grunt in either exertion or pain.

The haze seemed to thicken, to fill the room and choke him. Or was it the arm around his neck that was choking the breath from him? He couldn't tell. He felt the pistol taken from him and the woman's eyes upon him, staring at his face, frowning slightly as darkness veiled her from him.

He heard words: "We are compromised." And then nothing.

Valiantine sat up. Looking around he saw he was alone, lying on the mountainside as if he'd simply been tired and taken a nap.

Daylight. He guessed it to be late morning, by the position of the sun in the sky.

Leaping up, Valiantine caught himself from falling back down. He touched his head and his scalp and found quite a bit of dried blood. And Cabot. He'd lost his partner, too.

Why had he not been taken prisoner, he wondered, or killed outright for that matter? Unless there was some reason that he, and he hoped Cabot, were not to be held or murdered by those in the tower?

He began to run from the spot where he lay, but forced himself to stop and focus his thoughts. He'd been robbed of time, precious time, and he groaned inwardly at all that may have transpired since their encounter at the tower.

The tower. It appeared in his brain like a thunderbolt from Zeus. Looking around, Valiantine observed the landscape, trying to determine where exactly on Massanutten he was, and if he could find his way back to the tower. After a moment, he felt fairly certain he knew the way. His memory was good for landmarks, a trait that served him well in his duties as a covert agent for the United States Army.

Cabot. Where the hell was he, though?

Sickened at being overwhelmed by outside forces once again and by losing time, the lieutenant stalked off, his eyes searching for the path up the mountain.

Making his way through a copse of trees, he heard voices somewhere ahead of him. Nearing their source, he crept up on the spot to see several figures menacing a lone man.

Agent Cabot was down on one knee, his back to a large rock. Before him, some twenty feet away, stood a group of twelve men. They appeared to be uniformed soldiers, at first glance, but it all felt very, very wrong to Valiantine.

The men wore no insignia of any kind, though their uniforms vaguely resembled those of the United States Army. They were made from a strange, black cloth that, again, resembled one of the types the agents had uncovered on their last mission. Some of the men wore caps, while others went bareheaded; in all, Valiantine thought them very sloppy.

He also believed them to be an opposing faction, another piece to the confounding puzzle of the airships.

The lieutenant could hear Cabot speaking, saying that he'd just fallen asleep, that he meant no harm to the men. A few of the soldiers grinned, looking at each other with somewhat bored expressions. Thankfully, thought Valiantine, none of them had drawn their weapons on his partner. Not yet.

He stepped from between two trees and into the open. The soldiers wheeled around to look at him. The lieutenant saw hands reaching for pistols and rifles, but again, they seemed to restrain themselves.

"Gentlemen, my friend and I," he said, indicating Cabot, "have no quarrel with you. In fact, we have something I trust you want."

"Is this wise?"

Valiantine glanced over at his partner, but kept walking.

"I am angry, Cabot," he said out of the corner of his mouth. "I am angry at being manipulated throughout this investigation. I would think you'd be angry, too."

They walked shoulder to shoulder over the path to the tower, passing the spot where they'd encountered the man-creature and Valiantine had been wounded. His scalp prickled at the thought.

"I am," Cabot replied, "but it may be foolhardy to set these . . . men loose on that tower. We have no idea what—"

"Exactly," Valiantine interjected. "We have *no idea* of any of this, Cabot, save that these soldiers or whatever they are seem to be in opposition to those people in the tower. I intend to set a flame to the tinderbox and see what comes of it. Then, perhaps, we will have some idea of what we have been involved with all this time."

The lieutenant's plan was a simple one: lead the group to the tower and allow them to do the agents' work for them. He'd played one faction against another in the past, in his missions to other countries, and if one thing remained constant throughout such action it was that he always got results.

He almost ached to see the results of his present plan.

If Cabot disagreed, he held his counsel. Valiantine assumed the man's silence to be his agreement, so they trudged ahead, leading the small troop of strange figures onward toward their goal.

"See here," he said, indicating broken limbs in a tangle of foliage. "Here is where we crashed through to get away from that thing that attacked us. We are on the right track."

Though it was noon or very nearly so, the sunlight had waned and the air had grown hazy. Both agents recognized the signs.

"The vapor," Cabot said, glancing over his shoulder at the soldiers walking in loose formation behind them. "That damnable gas. It has many purposes, apparently."

Valiantine nodded, kept walking. "Yes, but what is its source? That stone from the heavens, in Carnavon's shed . . . it seemed to produce the vapor, but it was destroyed. Destroyed by the airship. Why would they do that, if the meteorite . . . ?"

"There!" one of the soldiers shouted, and Valiantine looked up to see the tower before them. Or what could be seen of it through the heavy fog that gripped it like a giant fist.

The dense cloud all but obscured the structure, completely blanketing its crown and the metal dome there. Below, the base of the tower could still be seen, but just barely. Above, where the dome should be, the two agents heard a creaking sound, like wood rubbing against wood, and voices, faint but evident.

"Dammit! It's here, Cabot! It's *here!*"

No sooner had the words left Valiantine's lips than came the distinct sound of a pistol being cocked at the back of his head.

"While we appreciate your service to us, sir," the soldier said, pressing the weapon against his skull, "we have our orders. You will take it like men, won't you?"

The lieutenant did not try to turn around, but watched as the rest of the troop, ten soldiers, deployed themselves around the entrance to the tower. Inside, he seethed.

"We've come a long way," Valiantine told his would-be executioner. "We've been presented with a mystery, like none other I've ever known. Surely you will allow us to know—"

"No," the soldier said. "No, I'm afraid not. We're on a time-table here; yours is done. You've reached the end of it, sir."

He brought his heavy hiking boot down upon the soldier's own boot, a sickening crunching sound his reward for the force with which he delivered it. The man screamed and Valiantine swung around to drive a fist into his face.

Cabot had smashed his own executioner's kneecap. *Just as effective*, thought the lieutenant.

He looked up to see that the other soldiers had moved on and already entered the tower, presumably continuing their mission while Valiantine and Cabot were being dealt with by their fellows.

"Cabot!" he said, looking up at the obscured dome far above them. There lay all their answers, but it might have been an ocean's length away for all the good it did them at the moment.

"Where to?" his partner asked, having dispatched his assailant.

Valiantine's mouth tightened into a straight line across his weary, blood-streaked face.

"Up. We go up."

Inside, a small battle was being waged.

The two agents made their way through the door, wary of the

fight before them. The vapor had almost completely covered the room, but they could hear the sounds of life and death struggles echoing from wall to wall.

A gunshot sounded; someone screamed. Valiantine turned to Cabot to urge him to keep his head down, but the Treasury man had left his side and was making his way around the room, hugging the wall. The Army man was about to demand to know what he was doing, but he suddenly realized what Cabot was up to.

"Godspeed, and be safe," he whispered. Looking around, he found the base of the staircase up to the tower and made for it.

Out of the fog stumbled the woman, she of the sultry voice and cold eyes. One sleeve of her garment had been torn away, her arm slashed to ribbons. She appeared to look at Valiantine, but he saw that she had been shot in the temple, her movements merely some autonomic function. Her lifeless form slumped to ground in front of him.

Leaping over the body, he alighted on the first step of the stairs and began to climb.

The sounds of the battle below him grew louder; he had no idea who was winning, nor did he care. He felt cold inside, yet there was a fire in his legs, driving him upward.

Something made him glance to the floor of the room and at that moment, the mist parted and he saw Cabot standing in the corner of the room that was strewn with straw. There, on the straw, lay a large, dark figure, chained to the wall.

Valiantine paused to watch as Cabot pointed a pistol at the prone figure and delivered a bullet into its brain.

He continued upward.

The fog, the mist, the vapor . . . Whatever the devilish element was, it clung to him, an almost tangible thing that threatened to lift him up and dash him down the stairs. He resisted the thoughts that came to him, that it was a living entity, one that could stop him if it so desired.

More than halfway up the tower, or what he assumed to be halfway, Valiantine heard voices above him. He looked up into the mist to see a face hanging there, staring down at him with simmering fury.

The bandit, Awanai.

The lieutenant reached for his pistol, forgetting that he had lost it somehow. Instead, he gripped the railing of the staircase and prepared to propel himself upward.

"Damn you!" he screeched at the Oriental face. "What is this all about? Tell me! Dammit, tell me!"

The round muzzle of a pistol poked out through the vapors below the reddening face, like a third eye. Valiantine tensed, ready to take the bullet if he had to.

A voice called out from above Awanai, splitting the tension right down the middle.

"Come! We are going!"

Distracted, Awanai turned to look for the speaker.

Valiantine shot up the stairs like a cannonball and leapt at the bandit. In a split second, he was on the man, pummeling him with his fists, over and over again, hurling obscenities at him.

Awanai yelped in surprise and in pain. The pistol tumbled from his grip and fell over the railing to disappear into the mist. Valiantine got his hands around the bandit's throat and stared down into the man's rapidly bruising face.

"Valiantine!"

Cabot's shout from somewhere below sliced through his intensity, his overwhelming drive to choke the life from the bandit. Awanai seized the opportunity and drove a gloved fist into the lieutenant's stomach.

Valiantine fell back, his head hitting the railing and his body crashing down onto the stairs. He rolled, bouncing down the steps like a barrel loosened from a cart.

Down the stairs he tumbled, separated from his wits and hurling into the misty void.

The next thing Valiantine knew, he was being half-dragged, half-carried from the tower. There was shouting all around him, or so it seemed. Cabot's labored breathing sounded like a locomotive to which he'd strayed too close.

"No," he whispered. "Up. We must go up."

"Right now," Cabot answered, "we're getting away from that tower, Valiantine."

An explosion rocked the area, the very ground on which they stood. The lieutenant looked up from Cabot's grasp on him to see fire belching from the tower's doorway. Off to one side several figures ran from the scene and into the trees.

He pushed his partner away from him and stood silently, watching as the tower crumpled at its base, then fell in upon itself. The metal dome at its apex made a deafening, resounding crash as it came down upon the smoking, burning rubble of the ruined structure.

A shout pulled his attention off to the treeline. There, a soldier came jogging toward them, pointing a rifle at the two agents. Cabot raised his pistol and downed the man with a single shot to the head. Two figures ran out and scooped up their fallen comrade and carried him back into trees.

Valiantine did not wait to see if there were more challenges from the soldiers. Skirting the wreckage of the tower, he stalked off, Cabot shouting after him.

"You're not in your right mind," his partner told him as he caught up to him. "You're hurt. Most likely you're delirious . . ."

"Shut up," he told the Treasury man. "They're getting away."

"The soldiers? No, Valiantine; I believe they're already beyond us."

He spat on the ground at the mention of the troop of mystery men. "No, God damn them, not them. The airship, Cabot. The God damned *airship*."

Surprisingly, Cabot linked his arm with his, lending him his speed. Together, they raced around the wreckage of the tower and up the mountain.

Somewhere near the top of Massanutten, they came upon a clearing. The air there was clear of mist, the sky blue and peaceful.

Both men scanned the skies. Valiantine's heart pounded in his chest, drowning out his thoughts. He had only one desire; actual thoughts were unnecessary.

The skies were serene, but empty.

They stood there for several minutes, until Valiantine could stand no more and found a small grouping of rocks upon which to rest. Cabot stood at his side, looking over the lieutenant's head at the pleasing green of the trees around them.

Valiantine glanced up at his partner, who appeared as a silhouette against the sun. He was just about to speak to the man when something seemed to eject itself from Cabot's head and float across the sky.

"There!" he said, pointing.

Cabot twisted around to see what Valiantine was seeing.

A large, dark shape moved through the sky, slowly, but picking up speed. Valiantine reached out to Cabot to help him to his feet, to better view the object.

It was like looking up at the hull of a large sailing vessel, though neither man could determine its exact size nor how far away from them it was in the sky. The lieutenant shaded his eyes from the sun to try and discern more detail, but the object began to move even faster and turned away from them to obscure its length.

"It's immense," Cabot said.

Valiantine nodded in agreement, tears clouding his eyes, though a wry smile flitted across his face.

"It's Helios' chariot, Cabot. It's Icarus, but he's flying too close to the sun . . ."

The Treasury man eased his partner back down onto the rock, allowing Valiantine his babbling, his chaotic, troubled thoughts.

"Right then; where to now?"

Valiantine's question hung in the air between them as they sauntered down the main street of Luray and past the telegraph office. The door to the establishment opened as they passed and a young boy exited, looking all around.

"'Scuse me, sir," the boy said. "Are you . . ." He looked down at the envelope in his hand. ". . . 'Lieutenant Michael Valentine'?"

Valiantine stared at Cabot, ignoring the usual mispronunciation of his name and wondering over the amazing event of someone knowing where he was at the moment.

The telegram produced an answer, one that chilled him.

"'Stay where you are. Wellington,'" he read off the telegram.

"Good Lord!" Cabot said. "How?"

Both men felt suddenly very exposed and made their way off the street and onto the porch of a nearby tavern. Across the way, a train had pulled into the station and its passengers began to disembark.

"I'm afraid I'm at a loss for words, Cabot. This is impossible."

The Treasury man grinned slightly, though darkly. "The impossible is what we traffic in these days, Valiantine. I don't know why I'm even surprised at all."

"This should surprise you, then," his partner said, nodding in the direction of the train station. Cabot looked across the street to behold three men who had just stepped down from the train.

"Wellington . . . !" Valiantine said.

"And Assistant Director Gallows," Cabot observed. "But the third man . . . ?"

Almost a giant, with wide, square shoulders, a massive jaw, and thick, wavy black hair, the man's eyes scanned the platform, his hand gripping a massive wooden cane with a silver top.

"I'm assuming," Valiantine said, stepping backwards into the shadows cast by the porch's roof, "that he is our mystery 'Executive Director,' Barnaby Scarborough. This has become quite a tangle."

"I've no desire to talk with them, or be spoken to by them," Cabot said.

"Too late to leave by coach," Valiantine observed, whipping

his head back and forth, seeking an escape route. "The train . . . wherever it may take us."

The two agents exited quickly through the rear of the tavern and made their way by a circuitous path along back streets to the train station. Once onboard the train, they settled into seats and looked all about them to see if they'd been noticed.

As the train began to chug away from the station, Valiantine looked out the window to see Wellington rush onto the platform and peer at the departing train, his face livid. A half-second later, Gallows and the man they presumed to be Scarborough appeared, too.

Valiantine suppressed an urge to lean out from his window and wave.

MAPS AND PLANS
Duane Spurlock

October 1897

W hy are we here?"

Cabot watched Valiantine sip coffee and shrug his shoulders. "Consider it a strategic retreat," the lieutenant said.

"We've been kicked off the case we were purposefully chosen for. To our knowledge, no one else is working on this investigation. This is no retreat from a battle. We were dismissed. And, we're hiding." He glared at Valiantine. Seeing no response, Cabot added, "In terms you might better understand, you are absent from duty without leave."

They sat over the remains of lunch in a Dayton chop house. Cabot frowned more deeply when he saw his partner shrug again.

Valiantine ignored Cabot's jab. "To lick our wounds? To plan?" the lieutenant suggested. "We set up headquarters here because the sightings occurred most often in the center of the country. But we've hardly been here since establishing the place."

Cabot slurped his own coffee.

Valiantine pointed a finger at him. "To be a bit more accurate, *we* are absent from duty without leave. But really, absent from *what* duty? We have been *relieved* of duty. Perhaps we *are* absent without telling our superiors where we are and what we are about. Enough of that."

"Enough? We fled our superiors! We fled—we fled a battle scene."

Valiantine's expression soured.

Cabot continued: "We witnessed a battle between two factions, foreign combatants on American soil! Leaving that behind, not reporting—isn't that like desertion?"

"I am not a deserter!" The lieutenant's anger boiled in the glare he directed at his partner.

Cabot raised a hand. He'd gone too far. "I'm sorry. I'm a bit worried. I'm not sure where we fit into all this. I'm not even sure what *all this* is. I *am* sure we're in some sort of trouble for running away from Gallows and Wellington."

"You think you're the only one worried?" Valiantine knotted his hands on the table. "I've dedicated my life to serving my country. I've lived by the rules and regulations of a professional military man in large and small conflicts for years. Don't you understand that leaving a battlefield—that was no retreat, we simply ran away. And we didn't report to our superior officers. I've responded to each of our recent encounters in the exact opposite manner to what I would expect of myself."

"You're right."

"That's enough!" Cabot watched the lieutenant's face. The signs of the fight going on in the man's mind were plainly evident in his rapidly changing expressions.

After a couple of minutes, Valiantine sighed and looked at Cabot. He appeared to have gained some control over his volatile emotions. "I apologize. I've followed orders, just as you have. And then I was told I was foolish to do so. I've worked to be a good soldier, and now I'm reacting as a bad soldier." He exhaled deeply. "I'm simply working from a place that is completely unfamiliar to me. I don't have the first idea about what should be the correct response to anything that's been told me recently."

Cabot nodded, but remained silent. He recognized his own conflicting emotions in his colleague's description.

Valiantine gave him a sharp look. "You're always talking

about the lessons you learned from Yankee Bligh. What would he do in this situation?"

The question made Cabot stop chewing his anger. "I haven't considered that."

Valiantine sat back in his chair. "We have plenty of time for it now."

The lieutenant's sudden nonchalance momentarily refreshed Cabot's irritation, but the Treasury agent chose to focus on Valiantine's suggestion. He tried to recall if his mentor had faced a similar situation.

"This isn't like any sort of case he might have been warned away from," Cabot said.

"Of course it is. We're investigating a mystery. We've been told to stop. And we've encountered every sort of strangeness in the mountains by Luray."

"Yes, I mean it's different. We weren't directed to investigate a crime, but a mystery."

"Mystery or not, crimes have been committed," Valiantine said.

Cabot sighed. "Yes." He poured more coffee. "I don't know if Yankee was ever told to stop working a case, but he told me, 'What does the *case* demand? Don't follow orders. Follow the case. Chase down the clues.'"

"Sounds good." Valiantine emptied his cup into his mouth. He stood up. "Let's get to work."

The agents had set up shop at the Atlas Hotel on the corner of Third and Ludlow. They had taken adjoining rooms on the third floor. The two rooms didn't have a connecting door, but one agent could knock on the wall to call to his partner.

A large map of the United States and its territories was tacked to a wall in Cabot's room. Pins tied with scraps of colored ribbon were stuck into the map.

"Let me say this aloud, and you correct me where I've gone astray," Cabot said. "There were no official reports on the airships before we started our investigations, only newspaper clippings. Those are represented by the blue pins."

"Are you sure those are all legitimate reports," Valiantine questioned, "and not a mixture of journalistic hyperbole and bad whiskey?"

"I've heard nothing different from Assistant Director Gallows. Had Wellington said anything to you?"

The lieutenant shook his head.

"Unless we travel to each of these sites—Sacramento, San Francisco, Omaha, and the others—and question people there, we won't know for sure. We could split up and do that, but I'm not sure we have that luxury."

"We certainly can't turn in travel expenses now. And I doubt we're being paid during our suspension."

Cabot reviewed a handwritten list of locations and dates. He frowned at the map.

"Sightings started in California. There were at least three last November. Nothing else until this past February, northeast to three sites in Nebraska: Hastings, then Inavale, and eleven days later over Omaha. South to Texas. North again to Kansas. Northeast to Iowa. South to Missouri. By April it traveled northeast again, arriving in Chicago. East to Kalamazoo by April 15."

Valiantine said, "Then in May, I saw it in Indiana—south—and you saw it again in Kansas—southwest."

"The red pins, those are us. That's a lot of territory covered in May."

"Do you think there's more than one airship?"

Cabot looked at his partner. He saw the sign of Valiantine's displeasure, the furrow above his nose.

"I suppose if there's one, it's possible there's another. Or it travels remarkably quickly."

"It wouldn't be slowed down by obstacles in the landscape," Valiantine said. "It would simply fly over hills or rivers. It wouldn't need roads or bridges." He tapped the knuckle of an index finger against his chin. "We have seen only one of the factions with an airship. I suppose it is possible only one of these groups has such a device."

Cabot returned his attention to the map. He gestured at the final three pins bearing bits of yellow ribbon. "And we encountered the airship in Detroit, Louisville, and near Luray."

"To the northeast, south, and then east."

Cabot remembered Yankee Bligh once drawing lines on a street map of Louisville as a method for determining a murderer's path. *If you know where someone's been, you maybe can figure out where he's going or where he's from*, he'd said at the time. Cabot plucked a ball of twine from atop a wash stand. He wound an end around the first blue pin representing Sacramento, advanced the twine to wind it on the San Francisco pin, and on to each of the following pins according to the dates on his list. Finally, he cut the twine with his Barlow knife and wound the loose end around the final pin. He tossed the ball to Valiantine. "A possible map of the airship's journeys."

"That shows a lot of zigging and zagging," the lieutenant said. "For what purpose? From a strategic perspective, a lot of time is spent on covering the same ground several times. From a military sense, that's very inefficient."

Cabot stared at Valiantine. "So, from that way of thinking, you're suggesting more than one airship seems likely. That one craft isn't tacking all over the countryside, but multiple ships are traveling different paths, in different parts of the country."

Valiantine frowned at the map again, then nodded and looked at Cabot. "That's a possibility. One traveling in the north, the other taking a southern route."

Cabot sighed and crossed his arms. "If we'd ever had a clear enough look at all of these sites to determine if there is more than one. That would help."

He took a step closer to the map. He stared at the path he'd marked. He wanted the pins and twine to reveal the map's secrets.

Nothing.

If Yankee Bligh had looked at this map, what would he have said?

Cabot remembered his mentor saying this: "A pile of lumber

and a pile of stone don't look like much until you put them together to build a house. A pile of clues doesn't look like anything until you put the parts together to see what they build."

Cabot faced Valiantine and raised a finger. "Perhaps two ships. But we don't know. So maybe there is only one ship. If so, we don't know why it zigs and zags. But we can guess: maybe it's chasing someone."

He saw the furrow disappear from Valiantine's brow as the lieutenant considered the proposition.

"Or," Valiantine said, "it's being chased."

"Ah." Cabot spun back to the map. "Two possibilities for one airship. I'll buy a lighter or darker twine later, and maybe we can come up with two separate paths that follow your proposal for two ships." He reached and lightly touched one pin head, then another. "We still don't know why they are showing up in these places."

"Maybe it was just spotted in each location on its way to somewhere else?"

"That's possible, yes. But you said the fellow you met in Indiana had seen the ship more than once, correct?"

"Yes. And I saw it there, so it was staying in that location for some reason." Valiantine's frown was back. "Did anyone other than you see it in Kansas?"

"My questioning didn't turn up anyone who said so." Cabot took up a ladder-back chair and arranged it so he could sit and look at the map. Valiantine brought another chair from the other side of the room and did the same. The two men sat side by side.

Valiantine rubbed his chin. "We know the ship arrived in Detroit to destroy the factory and the meteor. Its purpose for appearing there seems obvious."

"And you saw this fellow Awanai both there and in Indiana. So there is some link there." Cabot felt constricted by the mystery facing them—he wanted to unravel its threads as he had unwound the twine. Even his throat felt tight. He noticed that not only had he crossed his arms, but his legs were crossed at the knees. He put both feet on the floor and placed his hands on his thighs. *You are not the case*, he remembered Yankee Bligh saying. But that wasn't completely true in this situation: Cabot and Valiantine had been in peril from injury and death during their encounters with the airships; and now their superiors had suspended them from the investigation.

He took a long, deep breath and focused a few moments on relaxing.

Once his mind felt a little clearer, Cabot asked aloud, "All right, Awanai showed up at three of these sites. What else do these places have in common?"

Valiantine tapped him on the arm. "Your coins. And those . . . beasts."

A thief in Indiana named Awanai. Gold coins that supposedly didn't exist and had a tendency to disappear. And murderous monster men.

The youthful features Cabot had seen on the creature in the Ohio River flashed before his mind's eye, but he swept away the image when he pushed up from his chair.

"The coins give me an idea. I'm going downstairs to send some telegrams."

"We're essentially *personae non gratae* in Washington now."

Cabot waved away the warning. "I don't need the muscle of the federal government for these messages."

Valiantine stood also. "All right. I'll go buy some twine."

When Valiantine returned, Cabot was pacing a short path, back and forth, before the map. He had an empty cup in his hand, and he gestured to a pot on a tray resting on the bedside lamp table. "Coffee's there." He took a spindle of twine from the lieutenant and began to mark off two routes: one starting in San Francisco, the other starting from Sacramento. When done, Cabot crossed his arms and studied the map.

"Do you suppose they were constructed in California?" he asked.

"They," Valiantine said. "You're sure now there are two?"

"Based on the timing and the tracks, it makes more sense."

"Perhaps constructed there. But perhaps they just entered the country at that point," the lieutenant said. "It would be hard to conceal a construction project of that size, I'd think."

"Unless it were done near a boat works." Cabot cocked his head. "Or *at* a shipyard. But if they were built elsewhere, and entered the country there—where did they come from?"

Silence.

Cabot spoke up again. "If we associate the coins with the airships, we know—or think we know—one lingered in Kansas for several weeks. And your encounter in Indiana suggests it was in that region, including Chicago and Kalamazoo, for some time."

"Yes?"

"So there may be a base near those areas in Kansas and Indiana. Like we found outside Luray."

"Kansas is flat as a pancake. How would you hide something like that?"

Cabot nodded. "Flat for the most part, yes, but also sparsely populated. It could be done, but you're right. You'd have to find a very lonely spot to remain undetected."

"Lots of timbered and remote areas in Michigan to hide in," Valiantine said. "Or perhaps they might use an island in Lake Michigan."

A rapid knock interrupted the two. Cabot opened the door, and a bellhop handed him two envelopes. The agent tipped the messenger and dismissed him.

He opened the first note. "Responses to some of the messages I sent. The Chief of Police in Broken Toe, Kansas, has agreed to use his position to send queries to his counterparts in other states—where the ships have been sighted—and ask if strange coins have turned up there."

"Good idea. The other note?"

As Cabot read the second telegram, he felt a heaviness settle near his diaphragm. "Chief Taylor in Louisville. Replies the coin we left in his possession has disappeared. Replaced with a worthless slug. Just as happened to Chief Barker in Kansas."

Valiantine made a noise. "What makes these coins so valuable?"

"Enigmas and conundrums. I gave the other two Louisville coins to Gallows. He didn't say anything about the Kansas coin I'd already turned in. I wonder if he still has possession of any of them?"

Cabot watched a frown take over the lieutenant's face. Then Valiantine wagged a finger at him. "You got involved when you were sent to Kansas because of the coins. Not for a ship sighting."

"Yes."

"Does that mean something?"

Cabot considered. "As soon as I returned to the Treasury Department, I was transferred from being simply a Treasury agent to being a Secret Service agent."

"And we were partnered immediately after. As though a plan was already in place for our Aero-Marshal assignment—before either of us had turned in our reports."

Cabot nodded. "It's inconclusive—perhaps coincidental—but it looks like I was sent to investigate the coin report by Gallows while he already had knowledge about the airships."

"And, most likely, their connection to the coins."

"We were urged to get to work immediately."

"And then," Valiantine sighed, "our superiors put a sudden, inexplicable stop to our investigations. It doesn't make sense. The logic doesn't follow."

The spot of heaviness Cabot had felt now burned within his chest. "From appearances—it seems we've been manipulated from the start."

He saw Valiantine's frown slowly melt. He nodded. "It looks that way. We took our assignment, followed it—"

"And we've been dismissed from active duty because of it. We're being used as scapegoats."

"Scapegoats? For what purpose?"

Cabot noticed pain in his fingers. He unclenched his fists. He began to pace before the map again. "I'm not sure. But Gallows and Wellington must know. And perhaps this Scarborough, who sent the note to us in Louisville. Do you know anything about him?"

"Nothing. I've not met him or heard his name other than from that telegram. And we can only suppose it was Scarborough we saw with the other two in Luray." Valiantine scrubbed his face with his hands. "The way you're talking—it's as if we weren't really sent out to investigate a mystery. As if there was already a plan in place for us, and we've been following it as directed by someone who knows that plan. Certainly *we* don't know it. Is there some political agenda in place that encompasses our investigation? Something above the level of the Army and the Treasury Department? What the hell is going on?"

Cabot stopped pacing. He stared at the map and thought, *Stop thinking of these lines and pins as clues; think of them as a* plan. He heard Yankee Bligh's voice: *Use the lumber. Build the house.* "No one is going to tell us," Cabot said. "We'll have to find out ourselves."

Cabot spent the afternoon walking the city streets. He churned over and sifted through the pieces he knew about his and Valiantine's puzzle while he kept moving from block to block. He was only half-aware of the people and businesses he passed. The questions in his mind were more real to him than his surroundings.

A fellow hailed him from outside a shop. The sign over the door read *Wright Cycle Company.* "Young man, you have a frightful expression on your face."

Cabot realized the muscles in his face hurt. His frown was tight as a clenched fist. He paused and tried to relax.

The man continued speaking in a jovial manner: "You need some relief from your worries, so you don't wear out that shoe leather so fast." He gestured to one of the bicycles arranged along the wall of the building. "Pedal your way to relaxation and your destination," he urged.

Cabot examined the machine. "No, no thank you. But you've given me an idea." He continued on his way, a new bit of information added to the swirl in his brain.

Later he joined Valiantine for an evening meal.

As the lieutenant chewed, Cabot said, "Earlier, we were talking about how quickly the airship travels."

"Yes?"

"I passed a shop for bicycles today. I wondered if there might be some way of propelling the ship besides the wind."

Valiantine swallowed. "Such as?"

"Oh, I don't know. But if you can push two wheels with your feet on pedals, might you not push an airship similarly?"

"With pedals?"

"As I said, I have no idea. Maybe with a paddle wheel, like a steam boat?"

Valiantine snorted. "Sounds preposterous."

Cabot frowned. "I think *preposterous* is the common word for everything we've been chasing."

Valiantine returned to his meal. Cabot tucked in as well. Between bites, he said, "I don't think we can accomplish anything further here."

Valiantine nodded and swallowed. "But I'm not sure what we can do anywhere else." He ticked off points with his fingers: "We don't have the first clue about where to search for possible bases. It seems our superiors are immersed in a plot that may well bring bad tidings our way, and their appearance in Luray suggests that may happen sooner rather than later. Further, we've gotten between two factions that are violently opposed to one another, and the parties from both sides are willing to do us grievous or mortal harm."

He put down his hands and looked at Cabot. "Is there any silver lining to these clouds I've not enumerated?"

The younger agent dabbed at his mouth and dropped his napkin on the table. He smiled as he answered: "Yes. I've bought us tickets. We leave in an hour for the District of Columbia."

It was midnight. The car rocked. Over the noise of the wheels on the rails, Cabot could hear the snoring of those other passengers who had not purchased the luxuries of a Pullman car.

Neither he nor Valiantine had yet attempted to settle down for sleep. The lieutenant's fretting was obvious to his companion. "I still do not believe this is wise," Valiantine said. "And I must repeat that I am very displeased you put this plan into action without first consulting me."

Cabot nodded. "You're right. I was very impulsive. But as you said yourself, what else could we do in Dayton? We must be bold and strike at the heart of . . . well, of this conspiracy. If they are handling the investigation of the airship tower in person, we may well return to Washington before they do. And we can use that to our advantage."

The frown didn't leave Valiantine's face, but his words let Cabot know the lieutenant was considering them worthwhile. "I've been part of military campaigns that have used a—a bold strike, as you say. Doing so may well be unexpected."

He turned to Cabot. The frown was gone, but a look of concern still marked his expression. "Cabot, we've been under a strain since our dismissal. And the encounters in the mountains—" He touched the spot on his head where he'd been injured. "I saw you kill that wounded monster. I'm still not sure what happened to you in Louisville. Are you all right, man? Are you up to this?"

Cabot's head sank. He stared at the floor between his shod feet.

"In Kansas," he said, "there were murders, as I told you. People torn apart by beasts, as we've encountered."

"Yes, I know."

"There were also disappearances."

"Yes?"

"The children of murder victims. They have yet to be found."

"I see."

"I believe we found them."

"Us?"

"I shot the beast in Louisville, and it knocked me into the

river. I saw it. It was floating in the water, injured. It was massive. But its face—"

Valiantine remained silent.

"It was the face of a child. Frightened, hurt, bewildered. A boy's face."

"What?"

"The airships. Somehow they did it. Turned those children into beasts. Creatures that killed their own parents. Dear God, it's horrific."

Cabot realized he'd dug his nails into his legs. He released his grip and knitted his fingers together. "I killed that child."

Valiantine sputtered. "It was a nightmare creature! A beast!"

"It was a child!"

Valiantine shushed him as one of the sleepers in the car stirred.

Cabot spoke more quietly. "It was a child. Turned unwillingly into a monster that killed its own blood. It was a child that was frightened and . . . trying to escape the monsters that made it a beast. I'm convinced of that. And I killed him."

He looked at Valiantine. The lieutenant's mouth opened, but he uttered no words.

Cabot continued: "I killed the one in Luray. I was utterly repulsed by what had happened to that child that once had lived in Kansas. But at that moment my mind was a whirl—whether caused by the gas in the tower, or simply by the horror I felt when I looked at the thing. It was a child, but it was a monster. I recalled the sight of the bodies we found in Louisville, and I knew what it had tried to do to us on the mountain side. Honestly, I don't know even now if I pulled the trigger for mercy's sake or revenge."

He stood and went out to the platform between cars. The noise of the train's passage washed over him. He gripped the rail. He wished for the buffeting wind, the smell of the locomotive's smoke, and the roar of the train to dilute the turmoil wheeling through his mind.

Valiantine didn't join him.

ಌ ಌ ಌ

Cabot tipped Kentucky bourbon from a bottle into a glass and handed it to his companion. Jack Burnley had been in Gallows' anteroom the day Cabot had left for Kansas. The round-faced and red-haired Treasury agent thanked Cabot and raised the glass to his lips while Cabot poured his own drink.

The two sat on the porch of Burnley's boarding house. Cabot had brought the bottle, as he had occasionally done in the past. They could pass the time in rocking chairs in this way only after dark, when Burnley's landlady would not complain about the bad reputation her house might receive from passersby witnessing men openly drinking spirits at her front door.

Cabot had remained on the platform between train cars for more than an hour. During that time he had tamped down the fires that turned his guts to cinders—the combined rage and revulsion from what had been done to the children. He knew those feelings bubbled up from his anger at the fear he'd felt in Kansas when he'd been chased by the beast in the dark. He knew his anger was unreasonable, but he couldn't tame it. Between the time he had returned to his seat inside the car and the agents' arrival in Washington, Cabot's anger had changed into a fluttering pain behind his breast bone. He remained aware of it all the while he prepared for his visit to Burnley. He hoped his jovial colleague would provide information that would be useful to the Aero-Marshals' plans.

Cabot was aware he had to keep his emotions in check—otherwise, he could endanger his and Valiantine's efforts to uncover the plot directed by Gallows, Wellington, and the mysterious Scarborough.

"We've not seen you for some weeks," Burnley said, bringing Cabot back to the present.

"I've been on an extended investigation." Cabot made no mention of the Aero-Marshal designation or his assignment, suspecting no information about it had been shared with anyone outside of the two so-called marshals.

"We wondered."

"Director Gallows has sent no one else out for a long assignment like this?"

"No. Not since you left." Burnley extended his glass for a refill. "I've been working on files in the office the past three weeks. I wouldn't mind getting out, I'll tell you that."

Burnley's response assured Cabot his companion knew nothing about his strange assignment nor his current status.

"I have been gone awhile," Cabot said. "Bring me up to date on a few things. Have you heard of a fellow named Barnaby Scarborough?"

Burnley frowned. "Sounds familiar. Yes! He was in visiting old man Gallows just a few weeks ago. I was there when he came in."

"Really?"

Burnley nodded. "Rufus said he's some muckety-muck. No particular appointment, not elected, but apparently has the ear of McKinley."

"The President?"

"McKinley, President, same man, yes." Burnley sloshed his drink.

"How interesting."

Burnley shrugged. "Rufus says he's at the White House every day." Bourbon dribbled onto the man's trousers. "Maybe Gallows is getting a promotion. Say—if he does, maybe we'll all move up. So Rufus says." Burnley beamed at Cabot.

The latter poured more from the bottle into his friend's glass. "Good to think so."

"I think Rufus is tired of the Treasury. Or the work. Wants a change. Thinks Gallows might take him along to wherever his new posting might be. Y'know—" Burnley began to squint and emphasized his point by gesturing with his glass, "—Gallows hasn't been in his office in days. Maybe he's picking out a new office somewhere. Think he'll be on the Cabinet?"

"I don't know, my friend. But I'm sure he'll be somewhere there's a great deal of excitement."

ల ల ల

When Cabot left Burnley, his red-haired colleague was ready for slumber. His own drink was nearly untouched, and he tossed the contents of his glass into the flower beds edging the porch.

He stood now among a cluster of trees. Cabot's silhouette merged with the black trunks in the night's dark. He considered what he had learned.

His thoughts were interrupted by the sounds of steps approaching through the trees. He stood quietly. The sounds stopped.

A voice whispered: "Cabot?" Valiantine.

"Here."

The lieutenant came forward. He handed his partner a small parcel. "It was waiting at the Post Office, as you said. Under the name Delos Thurman."

"Excellent."

"Is there an actual Delos Thurman?"

"Yankee Bligh's first two names. You didn't suppose 'Yankee' was his real name, did you?"

"Hm. One never knows."

Cabot dropped the parcel into his coat pocket. "You have a light?"

Valiantine raised a small lantern. "You're armed?"

"Now, always."

"Let's go."

They set out. The Washington night was warm and muggy. Cabot blamed the close air for the sweat crawling along his ribs, not the anxiety burbling in his guts.

They avoided areas lit by lamps and stayed in the shadows most of the way. They stopped when their destination lay just fifty yards away.

The Treasury Building.

"No one is usually around by this time of night," Cabot said.

"No guards?"

"A single man on patrol. But I wonder if Gallows might have had reinforcements posted."

"Why?"

Cabot rubbed his chin. "Perhaps he considered we might come back here."

Valiantine gave him a steady look. "This is our bold move. It's bold by the very fact that it's unlikely."

After a pause, Cabot nodded. "Posting more guards would only draw attention to Gallows. From what we've seen, he and the others want no more notice brought their way than is necessary. You're right."

"Is there a service entrance, some way to enter without being seen?"

"A service entrance, yes, but padlocked from inside."

"So?"

"So we use the front door." Cabot pointed. "There goes the guard."

A figure crossed the front of the building and continued into the darkness, lighting his way with a lantern.

The lieutenant adjusted the lamp he carried, got the light going. "All right."

Cabot opened the parcel Valiantine had brought. He stuffed the wrapping into one pocket of his jacket, and the contents of the parcel—a leather wallet—into the other side pocket. "All right."

The two agents walked toward the building and made their way directly to the front door. Cabot grasped the large pull and tugged. The door swung open. "The public trust."

They entered the public part of the building. Cabot led the way over a railing into a more private section, then ascended a stairway. Valiantine stayed close behind.

The two passed through a door at the top of the stairs, then down a hall. Valiantine's lamp lit their way.

Cabot stopped before one of the heavy doors that interrupted the undecorated walls every several yards. He unlocked it using a key from his vest pocket. They entered the anteroom of Gallows' office. Cabot took note of the desks where Jack Burnley, Rufus

Turner, and James Barnes had been busy the day he had left for Kansas: all sat in a line, and the top of each was clear of all papers and files.

The door at the other side of the room blocked the way to Gallows' office. Valiantine directed light on the ornate knob and lock.

Cabot tried the knob.

Locked.

He shrugged, then pulled the leather wallet from his jacket pocket. "This came from Sebastian Konz, my Louisville gunsmith. He's quite the craftsman—he's been awarded three or four patents for his inventions." Unfolded, the wallet revealed a number of key-shaped implements. Cabot plucked one after the other and tried each in the door's keyhole. Finally, he turned one of them with a satisfying *clunk*.

The two agents shared a look. Cabot turned the knob and entered.

Valiantine made the light dart around the office. "What are we looking for?" He followed his partner deeper into the room.

"I'm not sure yet." Cabot went behind Gallows' large desk. He relied on his wallet of implements again, working on the locked desk drawers. As he succeeded in unlocking each, he would open it and search its contents.

"No papers in here that mention anything we've been up to. Nothing that names Wellington or Scarborough."

Valiantine turned the light onto a large black safe that sat against the back wall of the room. "Is that next?"

"I suppose so."

The two approached the squat iron beast. "No keyhole," Valiantine said. "We've run out of luck here."

"Not necessarily." Cabot tucked the wallet back into his pocket then hunkered down in front of the safe's door. "Let me get the dial set to zero, then turn the lamp away. The dark will help me concentrate on my hearing."

"Your hearing?"

"I'll have my ear to the door, listening for tumblers falling."

Valiantine turned the lamp away from the safe. "You are full of surprising talents."

"As a police detective, one is in the company of an array of incorrigible people with a remarkable list of skills. One learns where and when one can." He put his ear to the metal door. "As a Treasury agent, the skills one hones are more narrowly focused because of the types of crimes one encounters, but the varieties are just as extraordinary."

"No doubt."

"Now shush."

Cabot tried not to strain to hear anything within the door's works—that might lead to hearing false *snicks* or *clicks* that would only cause his efforts to take longer. He closed his eyes and took a deep breath, then exhaled slowly. *Relax*, he thought. *Darken the mind like this room. Listen. Just listen, don't strain for what's not there. Caress the lock, and she will give up her whispers and giggles.*

He put his fingers on the dial. *Lightly, lightly*, he reminded himself. *We're here in the dark, the two of us, alone, quiet, and tender.*

Cabot began to turn the dial gently. Slowly. *Savor the tactile delights—the slight resistance of the turning, the whisper of its well-oiled glide, the press of the door's face against the cheek and the rising warmth there.*

Delicate, so delicate. Tell me your secrets, my dear.

Crick.

How sweet, how modest. Cabot began to turn the dial the opposite direction. *Careful, sir, no need to rush. Slow the breathing. Consider, no, relish the moment, the now, not the prize that awaits.*

Cabot continued his silent efforts. He lost track of time, living only for the instants when the tumblers spoke to him. Any sense of Valiantine's presence faded from his awareness. He turned the dial and listened, listened, until . . .

T-clack.

Oh, my dear.

Cabot took his fingers from the dial and grasped the door handle.

He turned the latch.

Thunk. "Ah. The light, please."

Valiantine quickly complied. In the yellow gleam, Cabot stood before the open door of the safe.

"Cabot, that's—that's amazing!"

"Perhaps. Primarily it is very tiring. Take a look in there, will you, while I catch my breath."

Valiantine stepped forward as Cabot stepped back. "Really, I am very impressed. How did you do that?"

"I had a good teacher," Cabot answered. "He said, 'Think of the safe as if it is a woman. You must be patient and gentle and kind. Especially patient. And then she will be yours.' What do you find?"

"Some currency—it will take your eye instead of mine to determine whether it's genuine or fake. Papers. But nothing about our investigations, and I don't see Wellington or Scarborough's name on anything here."

"Nothing else?" Cabot's spirits slumped.

"A velvet bag. Here. Did you say Gallows put the coin in a wooden box?"

"Yes!"

"Then here we may be." Valiantine drew three wooden boxes from a black drawstring bag and arranged them on Gallows' desk. In a snap they were open, and the lamp shone on the coin within each.

Cabot caught his breath. "That's them! Not all, I think, but perhaps he doesn't have them all."

He bent closer to examine the coins' details. "Odd," he said.

"What's that?"

"I can't tell which is the one I found in Kansas. Maybe none is. But they all seem far more worn than the ones I've seen so far."

"The same type of coin as the ones you've seen?"

"Oh, yes. And I can just make out the dates—again, same age as the ones I had in my hands. But they look so much older, worn down." Cabot reached out and touched the dull surface of one of the coins. "By Gadfrey!"

"What?"

"Look—just my touch seems to have . . . smudged the raised surface of the coin, marred the design. And here, my fingertip: it's shiny, as though the metal was turning to dust and lifted from the money onto my skin."

"Is it really gold?"

"Yes, yes, I'd swear so. But the coin seems to be . . . I'm not sure. Decaying? I've never seen anything like that before."

"Do you suppose they are—it sounds completely fantastic even to me as I say it—turning into slugs like the others that were found by the police?"

"I suppose that is possible—we certainly have reached the point where 'fantastic' means something different now than what it did several weeks ago. I had thought someone had stolen the other coins, replaced them with slugs. Perhaps one faction stealing from the other, or the original owners attempting to steal back clues they had accidentally left behind. But one metal degrading into another like that? It still seems rather unlikely."

Valiantine tapped a finger against Cabot's shoulder. "Diamonds come from coal, I hear."

"But that requires . . . geological time. These coins have only been around a few weeks."

"Certainly it's beyond my understanding. What next?"

Cabot closed the boxes and handed one to Valiantine. "Take this one. I'll take the others." He put a box in each of his jacket pockets. "Return the bag to the safe, then we'll close her up and be on our way."

"But what will we do with them? How do they help us? We still don't know anything further about the plot, if there is one, what our superiors have to do with any of this . . ."

"I don't know," Cabot said. "Perhaps we can use the coins as some sort of leverage, find out what's going on. But there's nothing else here we can use. Let's clean up and leave."

As they swept the room for signs of their entry and search, Valiantine said, "Cabot, I want to say—I'm sorry about that outburst. On the train. You've been through a great strain."

"Forget it."

"But you can't. It will be there, always. I'm a military man. I've experienced terrible battles, seen men do horrific things to other men. They come back when I least expect. Waiting for my eyes to close, for a relaxing moment in the sun, a drowsy afternoon while I'm gazing at leaves moving in a breeze." They were standing by the door. He gripped Cabot's arm. "I'm sorry, my friend."

Cabot nodded, then he gestured toward the door. "Let's go."

He locked Gallows' office door behind them, and did the same to the anteroom door. The two retraced their steps along the hall to the door at the top of the stairway. They paused to listen for sounds of any other movements before descending. Over the rail. To the door. Valiantine doused the lamp. Cabot cracked open the door.

He opened it a bit farther. "Clear."

The two men slipped out the door and were down the steps and heading back for the trees in moments.

A voice stopped them in their tracks: "Gentlemen, I am surprised to see you remaining so diligent about your duties even when you have been suspended from them." Gallows' voice.

The Aero-Marshals turned. Gallows and another figure were approaching from the shadows at the near corner of the building. The second spoke: "I told you, sir. I saw Cabot on Burnley's porch, then I followed him here. I kept an eye out for him, just as you asked."

"Yes, you did well, Mr. Turner."

Cabot's flight reflex was pushed aside by a sudden fury. "Rufus, you ambitious, preening bastard. Get out of this. Now."

Gallows stopped a dozen feet away. "Mr. Cabot, that is hardly the professional demeanor I would have expected from you. Particularly toward a colleague."

Turner stood a couple of feet behind and to the left of Gallows. Light from a distant lamp gave his sandy hair the look of brown smoke. A timid smile twitched across his lips.

"I'm not sure what you are about," Gallows said. "But it is just as well you are here."

Valiantine whispered, "Cabot, a wise retreat is in order."

Cabot was tired of running from his anger, his fears, the mysteries that whirled just out of reach. He refused to listen to the lieutenant's counsel. "What's going on here, Director? We're not sure what you're about, either."

"You're very bold, Cabot," Turner taunted.

Cabot released his venom: "As are you, Rufus, behind another man's skirts."

Gallows tutted. "My goodness, Mr. Cabot, your time in the frontier has done you no good turn."

Cabot felt the leash to his anger fall away. He leapt upon Gallows bodily, a growl rolling from his throat. The older man fell back, Cabot upon him.

Turner squawked and danced backward as Cabot pummeled Gallows' face and body with all his might. His fury fused with his frustration and powered his fists as he thumped his former superior. Gallows did not cry out, but grunted and groaned as he was thrashed.

Valiantine had dropped the lamp and clawed at Cabot's shoulders, trying to pull his partner off the older man. But the younger agent's rage kept him wiggling from the lieutenant's grasp, and he continued to pound Gallows' face, ribs and chest.

Finally Cabot began to tire, and Valiantine succeeded in untangling his partner from atop Gallows. He got Cabot to his feet. The younger agent's chest heaved. He looked down at Gallows and his sight seemed to clear. The man's face was a bloody mess. The Director groaned a long, rolling moan like someone trying to wake from a nightmare. Turner stood a yard away, his feet moving here and there, clearly unsure whether he should help Gallows or flee.

Cabot heard Valiantine's voice in his ear: "He wasn't fighting back. He wanted to keep us here. It was a delaying action. We must leave. *Now.*"

Cabot wheezed, "Damn." Valiantine turned him around and got his partner stumbling toward the deeper shadows under the trees.

Then the shadows moved. The trunks of the trees seemed to walk toward the two agents. The darkness separated and the moving figures were men in uniform.

"It's them," Cabot said.

They wore uniforms like those of the first victim they had found in Louisville. There were at least twenty of them, all armed with rifles.

Cabot turned to the left, Valiantine to the right. More of them were appearing from the shadows. The two agents were ringed in.

Cabot shook his head, still angry but now exhausted. "I'm sorry, Valiantine. I'm sorry."

The guards halted. In their circle were the Aero-Marshals and Turner.

The latter spoke up: "What is all this? Who are these men?"

Two more figures advanced at a stately pace from under the trees. They took their place in the circle of soldiers: Wellington and the third man the agents had seen getting off the train in Luray.

The latter gestured, and one of the soldiers fired. The sound was a shock to Cabot's nerves, and his knees nearly gave way. But the greater surprise was seeing Turner collapse to the ground like a dropped bag of grain.

Two of the soldiers approached and helped Gallows to his feet. He slumped between them as they led him away into the darkness.

The third man stepped forward. Valiantine's rage was clear in his voice: "What the hell is this? Who are you people? What is going on here?"

The stranger smiled. "Lieutenant Valiantine, Agent Cabot. It is a pleasure finally to meet you. Please allow me to introduce myself. My name is Barnaby Scarborough. And you are my prisoners."

THE LAST HUNT
Jim Beard

October 1897

E verything was wrong.
 Valiantine's eyes flicked from spot to spot while in his mind he ticked off the list: dirt on boot, crease in trousers, button askew, hair on sleeve, crumb on seat. The list expanded as he identified spots, piling up around him with maddening speed.

Everything was out of place. Everything seemed alien to him.

Wrestling internally with his compulsions, he looked over at the chief source of his irritation, his so-called superior, Major Wellington.

After Valiantine and Cabot's capture at the Treasury building, they'd been divested of their pistols, handcuffed, and blindfolded. Later, they'd been made to sit in a cart for a few hours until the sun had come up and from there they'd been hustled onto a train, still blindfolded. It struck him the measure was more to keep them off-balance than from recognizing their surroundings; he himself had learned this tactic in the field, a valuable tool when dealing with insurgents and the like.

Perhaps that's what Cabot and I are now considered, he thought. *Insurgents. So be it.*

Though they were no longer armed rebels, they still harbored something of value, or something Valiantine hoped was of value.

While Cabot pummeled Gallows, he'd managed to slip the coins they'd taken from Gallows' safe into his right boot, silently blessing the distraction. They rested there, strangely warm against the side of his foot and, so far as he could divine, unknown to those he'd come to think of as the Trio.

Those thoughts served to distract him from his nervous tics. They'd gotten worse, as they always did when he was at rest, not engaged in movement or action or great mental concentration. While he and Cabot had been running hither and yon, hunting airships, his aberration was relatively quiet; now, in the present and under arrest, they began to manifest in ever growing waves. The stress of the situation, and the time to dwell upon it, did that.

The agents' blindfolds and, surprisingly, their handcuffs had been removed once the train had gotten underway, allowing them full view of that stressful situation. Wellington sat across from them and next to one of the uniformed soldiers. In nearby seats sat more of the soldiers, filling at least half the car; the remaining seats were occupied by men in suits, many of them with the appearance of importance or rank. There was no sign of Scarborough or Gallows.

At one end of the car, a quartet of musicians sat playing a tune from Berlioz.

No one but Wellington looked at Valiantine. The Army man fought down his compulsions and stared back at his former superior officer. The major looked pale, almost ghostly white, and Valiantine wondered why he hadn't noticed the man's condition before. It reminded him, for some reason, of the coins and their own degradation, and he wondered if there was some connection there.

"I'm envious of you, Cabot," he said, his eyes flicking over to his partner momentarily. He tried not to linger on the Treasury man's bruised and swollen hands, but forced himself to concentrate his thoughts.

"How's that?" Cabot asked, sullen.

Valiantine looked back to the major, locking eyes with him

again. "Envious of your opportunity and wherewithal to thrash your boss. I should like a similar chance to pummel our friend here."

One side of Cabot's mouth quirked up. "Shouldn't speak so of your superior, Valiantine. It's disrespectful of his office."

"Oh, he's not my superior," the lieutenant said in earnest, almost enjoying the smoldering, growing fire behind the major's eyes.

Cabot shrugged. "Your commanding officer, then. Whatever have you."

"No," Valiantine corrected, "what I meant was that this man is not Bertram Wellington. He's an imposter."

It had taken the lieutenant far too long to realize the truth of it, but he told himself there had been too many distractions along the way. Now, it was all too clear.

The train had been moving slowly as it left the city, but it began to pick up speed. Valiantine saw they were chugging northward. He guessed they might be headed to Baltimore, or even Philadelphia. But why?

The major sat forward suddenly, opened his mouth to speak, his eyes fiery but his face still cold and dead. A hand appeared on his shoulder, stilling him. Barnaby Scarborough.

The great granite block of a man stepped from one side of Wellington and, ousting the soldier there, sat down beside him facing the two agents. The major actually had to slide over a bit to accommodate Scarborough's massive frame. Valiantine studied the broad, rocky face, the wavy black hair, and the piercing blue eyes, as well as the man's ghostly pallor. The paleness of his skin matched that of the major, yet perhaps it was even more blanched; the Lieutenant fancied it was glowing from within, colorless and luminescent.

"You are both right and wrong, sir," Scarborough said, settling his cane between his legs. "But for our purposes, this *is* the Bertram Wellington you know." He indicated the major with a minute sideways jut of his huge jaw. Wellington glowered, frowning all the while. The musicians moved on to a Brahms melody.

Scarborough appraised the two agents, as if for the first time. "You've caused us many a problem for two men whose backgrounds and histories seemed to indicate loyalty to duty and only minor forays into, shall we say, divergent thinking. You were meant to be of little use to us, and so, with your gross misconduct, we have now found a greater part for you to play. Both of you."

Valiantine ignored a small blot of dried condiment on Scarborough's vest and returned the man's gaze. "That makes little or no sense. What conspiracy are you up to? Why this complete sham of 'Department A-13'? Why involve us at all, sending us out to investigate a thing of which you apparently possessed full knowledge?"

The large man squinted at the lieutenant, the pale skin at the corners of his eyes crinkling like waxed paper in a butcher's shop.

"No," he said. "No, I'm afraid we're not here to answer your questions, Lieutenant Valiantine. We're not some villains from your dime novels with ponderous explanations of our wretched schemes."

Cabot shifted beside Valiantine, and the lieutenant sensed his partner's growing frustrations. It was all very maddening, the two men who sat across from them, seemingly solid and real, yet untouchable in a way, owing to their positions in the District of Columbia. He wanted to reach out and smash their skulls together until nothing was left but a pulpy red mass of bone and tissue.

Scarborough smiled, but without mirth. He reminded the lieutenant of an albino reptile he'd once seen in a zoological garden.

"We are explorers," the man said, glancing at Wellington. "And, I suppose, scientists of a kind, too." He turned to skewer both agents in turn with his haunting eyes.

"Your world is not yet ready for what we offer. And so, we have been acclimating it to ours."

The enigmatic words chilled Valiantine. His head swam from the sheer senselessness of them, so much that he momentarily forgot his compulsions.

"And yet," Cabot said quietly, "someone opposes you."

The lieutenant saw the reaction his partner's words had on the two men. *The two villains of the piece*, he told himself, in spite of their high-minded talk. They reacted as if slapped across their faces.

Scarborough recovered swiftly; Wellington did not. The large man frowned, gripping his cane, lifting it, and lightly tamping it back down again on the floorboards. Valiantine thought he might try and batter them with it.

"You will be implicated in the death of Turner; we've seen to that," the Executive Director said. "And more. Much more."

Valiantine watched as Scarborough's eyes drifted heavenward. Cabot spoke again.

"I presume you're close to the President. Such proximity is dangerous to you, even for a snake. McKinley's not a fool; he'll find you out."

That produced a small glint in Scarborough's eyes. He leaned a bit in the Treasury man's direction, addressing him.

"Why don't you tell him all about it yourself, Agent Cabot?" he said with a slight grin. "Our new Commander in Chief is right here on this very train."

The coins in his boot had grown even warmer, or so Valiantine thought. Outside the railcar window, the landscape whisked by, but he paid it little attention.

Around the two agents, the passengers went about their own business with little or no notice of them. The musicians continued playing. It was all very surreal.

"You aim to assassinate him," the lieutenant said. "It's sheer madness."

Next to him Cabot shifted slightly; Valiantine sensed his partner's dismay, but also his focus. If he knew him at all, even after the short time they'd been together, the Treasury man was priming himself like a rifle, ready for business. *Good man*, he thought.

"No, Lieutenant," Scarborough said, staring at him coldly.

"Rather it's the culmination of much planning. With a bit of improvisation here and there, admittedly." He glanced at Wellington. To Valiantine's surprise, the major cocked his head to one side and spat onto the floorboards.

The Executive Director smiled. "Bertram's no admirer of the President, as you can see. So, he will die since he cannot be . . . replaced, and then we," he favored Wellington with another sideways look, "will join with our, ah, brothers in the center."

With those words, Scarborough smiled in a fashion that seemed to indicate some private joke or bit of humor.

The coins fairly burned against Valiantine's woolen sock, forcing him to flex his foot to move them to a less sensitive spot. He looked all around, but saw little in the way of hope. McKinley would be killed, and he and Cabot left to shoulder the blame.

It was beyond the pale of reason. The abject lunacy of it made his temples throb.

"There's one last thing," Wellington said, suddenly sitting forward and positioning himself only inches from the lieutenant. "Where are the coins you took?"

Valiantine almost yelped out loud as the objects in question abruptly burned at his foot like red-hot pokers. A large shadow fell across the window next to him and the train shuddered as the engineer or someone began to apply its brakes.

He assessed his superior's face. "You know, I've been quiet about it all along, but it's gnawed at me the entire time, Major. You have a spot of lint on your coat, just there."

Before Wellington could stop him, Valiantine reached out with one hand, fingers questing for the objectionable material. Just below the major's chin, the Army man curled his fingers into a fist and drove it into the man's throat with great force.

The train slammed to a halt. The shadow grew larger. Wellington gasped and gurgled, clutching at his Adam's apple, eyes rounded in shock and pain.

Cabot kicked out with one boot, smacking the very bottom of Scarborough's cane. The head of it toppled toward him and, deftly catching it, he knocked the big man's hands away in light-ning-fast succession and drove the stick into his face.

Scarborough's head whipped back, blood spraying from his nose. He howled in agony.

Valiantine clubbed Wellington down onto the floorboards and leapt from his seat. His partner had already moved into the aisle. Together, they flung themselves at the black-clad soldiers around them, Cabot wielding the cane like a war axe.

Committed to their course of action, the two agents waded into the fray. Valiantine dispatched one soldier easily with a firm uppercut to the jaw, the man taken almost completely by surprise. The next opponent benefited from the sight of the prisoner's attack on his fellow by steeling himself for the coming assault.

Valiantine pushed down with both hands upon the shoulders of two passengers who sat across from each other on the aisle and swung both feet up and into the soldier's chest. His momentum and the force of the blow sent the man flying backwards and into a group of suited gentlemen. They all toppled down into a clump of writhing arms and legs.

The quartet did not pause, but continued with their tunes.

Cabot battered at two soldiers simultaneously, swinging the stick with vigor and accuracy. Such was the unrelenting violence of the agent's play that his adversaries could not retaliate. Smacking one soldier on the side of his head with enough force to knock him back into a seat, with no hesitation Cabot shattered the cane against the other.

Flinging his insensate opponents from his path, he made a leap and a run for the door at the end of the car, joining Valiantine there and pushing through to the small landing just outside the door and between the railcar and its neighbor.

"I'm angry," Cabot said.

"As well you should be," Valiantine replied. "We have to—"

Cabot grabbed his partner's arm before he could continue and hauled him through the door of the next railcar. Slamming it shut, he locked it and urged Valiantine to talk as they moved.

The passengers in the car, apparently reporters or some such, turned to look at the two agents, already bewildered by the train's braking.

"You have to get to the President. We have to stop them," Valiantine said.

"Where are we?" Cabot asked, moving hurriedly down the aisle.

"Over water," Valiantine said, glancing out the windows. "From the width of it, I'd say the Susquehanna."

They stopped at the far door of the car. "We should both attend to McKinley," Cabot insisted.

"No," his partner answered. "The airship is here. Overhead. They mean to escape by it."

"How do you know that?"

"You saw the shadow. My foot is burning, too. No time for further explanation."

"If they mean to escape the train . . . oh, Lord."

"Yes," Valiantine said, "they intend on total destruction. The President, the train, its passengers. Go to him, protect him. I'll take the locomotive."

Cabot watched as the other agent opened the door to the next car and moved off their landing. Behind them, their opponents battered at the door to the car they'd exited and locked.

"Godspeed, Valiantine."

The lieutenant glanced back over his shoulder to see Cabot's legs disappearing up and between the cars. *He'll enjoy running along the tops*, he thought to himself, and ran off toward the train's engine wondering what in the hell might await him there.

Valiantine peered over the top of the coal tender at the cab of the stilled locomotive. A man there, dressed all in black with a high collar, whipped his head around, caught sight of him, and raised a pistol in his direction.

The bullet missed Valiantine by mere inches.

He dove off the railcar's landing and down onto the bridge

next to the track. The river far below beckoned to him. He could hear shouting and what sounded like grunts that fisticuffs might produce.

Hugging the tender, he slipped along its flank toward the cab. A head sprang out from the engineer's domain and produced a small yelp. Valiantine flattened himself against the coal car as another bullet tore past his chest.

In a split second he was underneath the tender and, making his way to its far side, prayed the shooter would not release the brake.

Exiting out from the underbelly of the car, he ran toward the engine with all his might. Reaching it, Valiantine hit the footstep at the cab's side and vaulted up into its maw. Every muscle in his body protested the action.

Two men dressed as soldiers gaped at him: one, the shooter, hanging down off the far side of the cab, the other clenching the front of the train engineer's uniform, one fist cocked and ready to strike again.

Valiantine kicked out at the legs of the shooter, knocking him from his precarious position and down onto the bridge. He swung his arm at the other soldier, aiming at his head, but connecting with the man's shoulder. Pain lanced up his arm, but his adversary grunted and released the engineer. The lieutenant leapt upon the soldier, pummeling him repeatedly.

A sound behind him indicated the shooter had returned to the cab. Valiantine swung his dance partner around in front of him. The man's forehead imploded from the bullet that ripped through it. The engineer wailed in terror.

Using the corpse as a ramrod, the lieutenant forced the shooter back and out from the cab. He heard the man hit the bridge, yelling out in distress.

Valiantine coldly threw the corpse he held down upon the prone figure of the soldier and leapt down from the cab to land beside the tangle of bodies. He snatched the pistol from the man's hand and fired one shot into his brain.

Looking back up at the cab, he addressed the horror-stricken engineer.

"What were they about to do?" he asked, climbing up to the platform with haste.

The man gestured, trembling, to the floor of the cab. There lay another dead man, the engineer's mate, and beside him a small, smoking canister. With the door to the fire hole swung open, it was obvious the soldiers' intent was to drop the device within.

Wrapping it gingerly in a handkerchief, Valiantine secured the item in his coat pocket and, wielding the pistol, leapt back down to the ground to run across the bridge, alongside the train.

"Stay there!" he yelled back at the engineer. "Touch nothing!"

Expecting to be shot at any moment now, the lieutenant scanned the cars for anything that might look like the President's quarters. He didn't know the new Chief Executive well, but assumed the man was not above traveling incognito when it suited him.

Who knows what lark the Trio set him upon? he asked himself. *They most likely had arranged everything, the entire excursion.*

Valiantine attempted to look up over the railcars, to the sky above them, hoping to catch a glimpse of an airship.

A sharp lance of sunlight shot out from behind something large that hung there in the air, blinding him.

He rubbed at his eyes, cursing violently from the solar assault. Black spots danced across his vision as he stumbled onward in his headlong rush to reach the President.

"Valiantine! Good God, what are you doing!"

Frowning deeply, he looked up at the spot on the backside of a railcar he approximated his partner to be.

"Looked up at the sky, Cabot, tried to see but the sun blinded me . . . oh, dammit all, never mind. Is the President safe?"

A hand clutched at him and hauled him up onto a platform. Finally in the shade, the Army man blinked several times and began to make out his surroundings. Cabot stood there, encircled by several men in dark suits with bowlers and moustaches and raised pistols.

"The President's men, his *real* men," Cabot assured him. "Gentlemen, my partner, Army Lieutenant Michael Valiantine."

"What the *hell's* going on?" Valiantine demanded, stumbling through the door of the car and into its interior.

"That is something I'd very much like to know myself, sir."

The agent looked up into the broad, unsmiling face of the President of the United States.

"Who are you? What's this all about?'

Valiantine glanced over at Cabot, who caught his eye and held it. The lieutenant blinked once, twice, then shrugged his shoulders. Remarkably, in unison fed by some form of unspoken communication, both men reached into their pockets very slowly and carefully, so as to not alarm the President's guards, and produced badges from their wallets. They held them up for McKinley to see.

"Aero-Marshals, Mr. President," Valiantine said. "Department A-13."

It wasn't until they presented their true bonafides that the President's countenance took on a look of confusion rather than anger. Valiantine and Cabot's earnest talk of their ordeal seemed to placate their Commander in Chief, enough that the man agreed to listen further to their story while the train got underway once more.

"I have a war brewing on the horizon, gentlemen," the President told the two agents. "And while the stories of these 'airships' had intrigued me, I was confident that the matter was being investigated and addressed so that I may focus my attention on Spain."

"You may have another war on your hands then, Mr. President," Valiantine said.

They told McKinley all they knew, after the President ushered many of his associates out of his private train compartment, retaining only a few of his closest and most trusted advisers.

Valiantine outlined the scope of his and Cabot's explorations and encounters, all the while fretting over the time that slipped by and the distance between them and the leaders of the conspiracy.

Though Valiantine guessed he might regret it later, he held back some of what he and his partner had learned on the train from Scarborough; there was no way to credit it or present it in any way that would not make them sound like lunatics.

"I met Barnaby Scarborough when I was Governor of Ohio," the President told the agents, "but he did not strike me at the time as a man with much ambition. Then, roughly a year ago, he seemed to change, become bolder, started espousing grand ideas. I welcomed him into my administration as a visionary."

Valiantine frowned, looking over at Cabot. "Major Wellington also changed, while I was away on leave. Everything's backwards now with him. Disconcerting. I should have realized something was terribly wrong in the beginning."

"Gallows, also, but perhaps not to the extent of the other two," Cabot added. "But, suffice to say, we know their stripes now. And that they aim to cause untold trouble for the nation."

"We shall band together ourselves to hunt them down, to bring them to justice," the President said with resolve. "I will write out the order now for their arrest, and any who serve them."

For the next twenty minutes, Valiantine and Cabot pleaded with the man to allow them to track down the Trio themselves. Only they, so they reasoned, knew enough of the conspirators' minds to find them, and a smaller hunting party might not alert their prey to being hunted and drive them further underground.

"Very well," McKinley said, looking back and forth between the two agents with steel in his eyes. "Tell me what you will need for your, ahem, expedition, and I will see that you have it."

Valiantine considered, but it was Cabot who spoke.

"Horses," he said.

They were granted their request on the border of Maryland and Delaware. The President had the trains stopped and sent men to procure two fine equine specimens from a nearby farm, then presented them to Valiantine and Cabot for their approval.

"I never want to ride another train in my life," the lieutenant opined as he mounted his horse. He had gained experience as a rider throughout his Army career, and felt at home in the saddle. He assumed Cabot also felt no unease at all with the arrangement, for it was the Treasury man himself who had read Valiantine's mind and made the request.

"Indeed," the younger man said as he climbed atop his own animal. "Where to now?"

Valiantine sighed, scanning the horizon. It was mid-day and the sun still beat down upon them. His eyes ached from the shaft of it that had burned him before and his hands trembled a bit.

"Scarborough made that remark about joining their 'brothers in the center.' I feel strongly that he meant Philadelphia— 'brotherly love' and all that. It must mean that."

Cabot nodded his agreement, but narrowed his eyes. "But how will we know once we arrive there? How will we find them?"

"By these." The lieutenant held up a small, cinched bag. "The coins will show us the way. They're reacting to the airship, somehow. Damn near burnt my foot off back there on the train. We will know very soon if we are on the right track, though I believe we are."

Cabot swung his horse around to point its nose toward the northeast. "They're desperate," he said matter-of-factly. "They could do anything at this juncture."

Valiantine smiled slightly. "And does your Yankee Bligh have any words of wisdom about such desperation?"

"'*Desperate men are a danger both to you and to themselves,*'" the Treasury man quoted as he cracked his reins and rode off.

"That's what I was afraid he'd say," Valiantine murmured as he urged his own horse on.

By pushing the horses, they crossed the upper reaches of the state of Delaware in under two hours. While they rode, they attempted to collate everything they knew to that point; Valiantine found the rhythm of his horse's gait to be conducive to thinking.

"They meant us to fail all along," Cabot called out over the sound of pounding hooves.

"Apparently," Valiantine agreed, chewing on the sour taste of it. "Made them look like they were doing something about the phenomenon to the President. We were cherry-picked for asses."

"Never mind that," Cabot said. "Think about the coins; the metal is unstable? So, the degradation of their composition somehow reacts strongly to more of the same metal?"

The lieutenant reached into his coat pocket and drew out the bag containing the coins. It was warm to the touch, perhaps slightly warmer than an hour before. His brain balked at it, but it was a mild impossibility compared to all else they'd been asked to accept and believe.

"They're definitely heating up again. A divining rod to lead us right to our friends."

"The vapor, the gas, is part of it?" Cabot asked, watching his horse closely for signs of fatigue.

His partner shrugged. "Of the coins? I don't know, but it figures into the bigger picture mightily, of that I'm certain. I suspect it powers the airships."

Cabot remained silent, as if mulling it over himself. Valiantine suddenly pulled back on his reins, bringing his animal to a stop beside a large gate, part of a long line of fencing that paralleled the road.

"Catch," he told his companion, and tossed the bag of coins to him. Cabot caught it with one hand. His eyes widened a bit by holding it a moment.

Valiantine pointed across a broad field that stretched away from them. Some distance away, a collection of buildings sat to the north. To the northeast they could see the outskirts of Philadelphia.

"I've a feeling about this," he said.

A low fog had settled down upon the ground around them,

but not the extra-normal variety they'd encountered too many times before; this looked to be a product of nature. Together, they drove their horses to vault the fence and they took off at a canter across the field and toward the buildings. The coins grew hotter within the cinched bag.

"Is this the place?" Cabot asked, eyeing the compound before them.

Valiantine nodded once, curtly, as he set the bag of coins down on the grass next to the fence they peered over. It was a low structure, serving more to define the property than as any sort of barrier to keep onlookers such as themselves from entering. The entire area looked almost deserted, with weeds growing up around the cobblestone walkways and buildings, and a general taint of disuse hanging in the foggy air.

The gigantic stone structure they surveyed was one of five, dark and foreboding, with massive chimneys and blackened windows. The fog parted here and there, intermittently, allowing the agents glimpses of its massive presence, and sounds emanated from within its walls, indicating some activity.

Cabot scanned the building's length, then its height, which extended to five stories of near-black brick, dark windows, and a huge, oddly hulking structure that encompassed the majority of its top; he could not divine its use or purpose through the choking fog.

He turned to his comrade. "Munitions. I smell a foundry."

Valiantine stared at the building without blinking. "I concur."

Cabot appeared to think for a moment. "Their armament. The cannons. They mean to—good Lord."

"Yes," Valiantine nodded, grimacing underneath his moustache, "I follow your reasoning and again agree. They mean to lay waste to something. Again."

The lieutenant began to walk. Pushing open a rickety gate, he moved through it like an automaton, his eyes never leaving the building before him. Cabot followed.

"The city? Philadelphia?"

"No. I would say not. They've just had their plot to kill the President foiled. They will be quite put out. No, they have bigger prey in mind, I'd wager."

Valiantine strode across the cobblestones and the weeds, heading for a large doorway set into the side of the factory. His steps were unsure, though he did not falter in his headlong movement.

"Washington, then," Cabot offered soberly. "Damn them, but it has to be the capital."

The lieutenant stopped and glanced over his shoulder at his partner with deadened eyes.

"Yes."

"Putting a halt to it won't be easy," Cabot said, standing at Valiantine's side, shoulder to shoulder. "They'll have numbers on their side, their soldiers, and weapons. They're desperate, as we've said. But they're no fools."

The younger agent looked down at his partner's arm, frowning.

"Valiantine, your hand. It's trembling."

"Nonsense."

"No, in fact, your quirks are worse than before."

"Quirks?"

Cabot sighed. "Yes, you're riddled with them. Your . . . drives, your compulsions; call them what you will, but they're overtaking you. Perhaps it's wise if we—"

"No," Valiantine said. "We move *now*, while we have them within our grasp."

He spun on Cabot, his face reddened and angry. "I'm sick to death of the hunt. Sick of chasing these phantoms." He pointed up at the building. "We go in there now, together, and put an end to it. Or I go in there alone and execute my duty."

"Of course," Cabot said quietly, yet firmly, extending a hand. "Together. There is no other way, you blasted idiot."

"There is another way, you know."

The two agents spun around to see a figure step out of the fog and toward them: Awanai the bandit.

Though the air around them was murky, Valiantine could discern the distinct muzzle of a Colt pointed in their direction.

"Should never have given you that hooch in Indiana, Michael," the man said, shaking his head. "Now you think yourself attached to me."

Valiantine stared coldly at the figure he'd run across through several states, but said nothing.

"Pistols, gentlemen," Awanai ordered with a minute twitch of his own weapon. "Let's have them."

The bandit looked as he had before, but there was a look of unease about him; the lieutenant guessed all was not well in the airship circle.

He and Cabot offered their pistols, but Awanai motioned to drop the guns on the ground. He instructed the agents to slide the weapons toward him with their feet.

"You believe you can keep us both from advancing on you?" Cabot asked.

The bandit's countenance hardened. "Why don't we just find out then, boy?" he replied, raising his Colt, cocking it, and pointing it directly at the Treasury agent's head.

"Why did you kill Andrew Carnavon?" Valiantine asked. "And why are you here, now?"

Without taking his eyes off Cabot, Awanai offered a sly grin on his Oriental face. "Heh. Ol' Barnaby said you wanted answers, but he's never big on supplying them."

"You're not like the others," Cabot opined.

"No, no I'm not," the bandit said, lowering the pistol to his waist, but still covering both men. He smiled. "I'm smarter than them. I brought them here. They wouldn't be here, on your world, if not for me."

Valiantine squeezed his eyes shut, wagging his head slightly. "Scarborough said that, too: 'your world.'" He popped his eyes open again. "What the devil do you mean by that? You told me you were born in Indiana, in Manitou. And what have you done with Mr. Perklee?"

Awanai furrowed his brow. "Hmm, I'd given you two more credit than I needed to. Thought you'd . . . but no, I can see I was wrong. Ah, well, there's no harm now in telling you that we're not from here, if Barnaby took no care in hiding it. And Perklee? Alive and well, yet under lock and key. He's still got quite a brain underneath all that drunkenness. He's still important to me."

"The vapors, the gas," Cabot said. "From your 'world,' I surmise? And a kind of power source?"

The bandit looked upon the younger agent as if seeing him for the first time, or in a new light. He scrutinized Cabot's face.

"Yes, and from yours, too, but we took care of that. Can't have you following us into the heavens. The loss of Carnavon knocks you from that path just fine.

"And by the way, I call it 'vox.'"

"You're murderers," Valiantine seethed, doubling his fists. "Cold-blooded killers. The deaths in Detroit alone will see you rot in Hell—"

"You didn't care much for my beasties, did you, Agent Cabot?" the bandit said, ignoring Valiantine.

At that particular moment, a band struck up a tune, unseen, but distinct in its surreal orchestration.

"Lieutenant Valiantine's correct, sir," Cabot said to Awanai. "A berth in Hell awaits you, and I shall see you there."

The scuffle, when it came, surprised them all.

Looking back on it later, Valiantine insisted it wasn't that the combatants were unaware of the coming fracas, but that each one had underestimated his opponent.

Cabot lashed out in deliberate fury, not unlike his attack on Superintendent Gallows. The lieutenant saw the shock on Awanai's face; the man had expected a reaction, but not the ferocity of it.

Valiantine hoped he and his partner would once again act in unspoken, unplanned tandem, but Cabot's lightning fast assault took him unaware. His guess was the younger man himself would never have expected the strength of his own actions.

The bandit's pistol discharged. Valiantine saw a spray of red around Cabot, who grunted in pain. He dove to the ground for his own weapon, but Awanai fell backward under Cabot's fists and his booted foot kicked the pistol across the cobblestones and out of quick reach. The lieutenant could not see Cabot's firearm in the fog.

Awanai's vicious curses cut through the air, but quickly changed to howls of pain. Valiantine leapt for the bandit's legs, hoping to knock him completely to the ground, but the melee was too chaotic for him to gain purchase.

He tumbled back onto his haunches, trying to make sense of the scrapping. Cabot was a demon released from a bottle; Valiantine worried for the young man's soul.

In the blink of an eye, the Colt appeared in Cabot's hand. Blood dripped from the side of his face where the bandit's bullet had torn across it. He pointed the weapon at Awanai. Valiantine bellowed for him to stop.

"For them," Cabot said, and squeezed the trigger.

The bullet entered the bandit's left eye and exited just behind his ear. The body spasmed, sprawling onto the cobblestones like the dead weight it now was.

Valiantine looked down at the pooling blood underneath Awanai's head, the man's one intact eye staring without life up into the foggy sky.

"So many questions," the lieutenant whispered to himself.

Glancing away from the corpse, he saw Cabot walking toward the doors of the building.

"The answers lie within, Valiantine. Come on. We have more work to do."

Valiantine, feeling very, very weary, retrieved his pistol and followed him inside the factory.

On the ground floor, they found furnaces and metalworks. Factory men, engrossed in their tasks, did not notice the two agents. The workers fashioned cannon shells, apparently, though the munitions looked odd, not at all like what Valiantine was used to seeing.

The thought of cannons made him twitch even more. He fought with himself, biting his lip until it bled and beating one fist against his leg, slowly and rhythmically.

Finding a stairwell, they stealthily ascended it. The upper floors of the building were almost empty, save for the strains of music that still wafted about. Valiantine couldn't place the tune, so focused was he on quelling his compulsion to straighten, to clean, to put things to right.

On what they believed to be the top floor of the factory, the stairwell ended in a large, barren room. Massive wood supports extended from floor to ceiling, but otherwise the area was empty; no furniture, and no people.

Across from the agents, was a normal-sized wooden door, set into a wall that appeared somewhat newer than those around it.

The music seemed to be coming from behind the door.

Cabot opened his mouth to speak. Valiantine raised one hand, stilling him.

"No, don't tell me what Yankee Bligh had to say about doors. Just open the blasted thing."

Cabot smiled, but that made him wince from the gunshot wound on his cheek.

"Valiantine, damn you," he said, placing a hand on his partner's shoulder, "I wasn't going to say any such thing."

"Nonsense," Valiantine replied, stepping toward the door and gripping his pistol tightly. "You can't help it; it's a compulsion."

Reaching out for the latch, he realized his quirks had quieted; he was in action, moving forward and not looking back.

Behind the door was a wooden staircase. They mounted it and arrived at another door at its top. There, they heard the music very clearly.

Opening the door carefully, albeit not slowly, the two agents looked out into another large room. Covered from floor to ceiling in rich, wood paneling of exquisite craftsmanship, Valiantine was immediately struck by the dichotomy between the chamber and the grimy factory below.

The room was occupied by several people, all of them dressed not unlike those in the Luray tower. In one corner, a musical group consisting of horns, violins, cellos, and a few other assorted instruments sat, playing as the people milled about the space.

Valiantine noticed charts on the walls, as well as maps of the United States and one of Mexico. Nearby sat a large table at which four people pored over a map of what looked to be, from the lieutenant's vantage point, Washington, D.C. Standing silently at attention along the walls, were men dressed like soldiers, clutching rifles.

The room spoke to him, two words only: nerve center.

In the middle of it all stood Gallows, looking none the worse for wear, save for skin nearly the color of milk. Again, Valiantine drew a comparison to the coins' loss of color and detail.

Even more eye-opening, the man's bruises were almost completely healed.

"Well, what was it, Carnavon?" Gallows said, not immediately glancing up from the papers he was in the middle of inspecting. "We have—"

"He's dead," said Valiantine.

Gallows looked up and into the faces of the two agents.

"Damn and blast," he wheezed. "Unbelievable."

"Yes," a voice rumbled from off to one side. "But it really shouldn't come as much surprise to us, these two."

Barnaby Scarborough shut a door behind him, one through which he had just come. Beside him stood Major Wellington. Both men wore the best poker faces Valiantine had ever seen; if they were startled at all by the agents' appearance in their midst, they hid it well.

"The worst thing we ever did to ourselves," Wellington told his fellows, "was to not kill them when we had ample opportunity."

"No," Valiantine said, finding his voice. "The worst thing you ever did to yourselves was putting us together in the first place."

"I can see that now." Scarborough grunted. "Seize them," he ordered his soldiers, and the black-clad men left their posts to advance on the two agents.

Not waiting to be approached, Valiantine put a bullet in the head of the nearest of them.

The other soldiers paused, looked back to their commanders. The Trio glanced at each other, then back to the intruders.

Scarborough scowled, his neutral expression cracking. "All right, Lieutenant! All right for the moment. Damn Carnavon and his inability to stay in one place for any sizeable amount of time . . ."

The Executive Director scowled all the more. After a moment's reflection, he spoke.

"Ah, well. Gentlemen, to our compatriot." He bowed his head and raised one hand. The band stopped playing. "Inventor, architect, explorer, visionary, a singular man in all respects. We owe him much, and I shall mourn him."

It was difficult for Valiantine to credit the demonstration, as surreal and dream-like as it was. He sensed sadness, yes, and resignation in the words, but also a small spike of thrill that Awanai—the Trio referred to him as "Carnavon" as if it were his real name—was no more. Why did it seem like they were moving in slow-motion? *Perhaps*, he told himself, the gas, *the "vox" the bandit referred to, is making them lethargic, somehow. And, as their lack of security indicates, sloppy.*

In a flash of insight, he guessed the constant music might exist to stir them, to keep these strange people alert.

"Are you finished?" he asked the Trio, repressing his musing. "Because you're going to answer our questions now."

One of the soldiers lifted his rifle. Cabot shot him down in the wink of an eye.

The Trio did not respond. Valiantine continued.

"How many airships are there?"

Silence.

"The coins?"

Scarborough chuckled low in his throat, mockingly. "Altered upon our arrival, as all of our metals were, seemingly. We did not realize it at first."

"Who is hunting you?"

"Why, our enemies, of course," the big man replied. "Yours, too, unfortunately for your world."

"Dammit," Cabot spat, "what does that *mean*? Where are you from?"

The Trio shifted, coming together in a single line, shoulder to shoulder, as if one massive figure.

"Elsewhere," Wellington said, his face deadpan, but his eyes dancing.

"Talk!" Valiantine shouted at the top of his lungs. "God damn you, *talk*!"

He raised his pistol and felled an approaching soldier, then another and another. Someone screamed, but he kept on shooting. Return fire from somewhere in the room splintered the wood paneling behind him, the bullets tearing past him, ripping at his coat and hair. *At last*, he thought, *I've prompted them into some action . . .*

"Up and out!" he heard Scarborough bellow above the din.

The room began to vibrate, the motion coming from deep within its wall. Underneath their feet, the floor danced, or seemed to.

"Vox release!" a voice yelled. Gas issued forth from the walls or ceiling, Valiantine couldn't tell which. He recognized it instantly as the vapor from the meteor. Items began to float toward the ceiling; he swore he saw boots and bodies lifting up from the floor.

As if to deny him the vision, the people in the room ran away from its center, reaching for doors, disappearing from view. The Trio was already gone.

Cabot shoved Valiantine out the door through which they entered the room. Though sorely desiring nothing more than to get his hands around Scarborough's throat, the lieutenant saw the sense in flight; he felt the effect of the vapors immediately and knew there was little they could do to fight it.

"They're destroying the building!" Cabot shouted as they ran. "And us with it!"

They tumbled down the stairs and into the empty fifth floor of the factory. Not pausing in their flight, the two men flew down the stairwell, trying to reach the building's main doors.

Around them, the entire structure shook and swayed, its bricks and beams vibrating as if made from paper.

They shouted warnings to the men in the foundry, but saw the metalworks were already abandoned. One giant bowl of molten, liquid metal began to tip as they watched, spilling its glowing contents out onto the surrounding floor and work stations, setting everything ablaze.

Valiantine and Cabot tore open the factory's doors and ran outside, hacking and coughing from the thick air they'd just left.

Loud, echoing booms exploded in their ears. Pieces of wood fell about them, narrowly missing their heads and limbs. Attempting to put some distance between themselves and the building, they finally turned to witness the structure's great, darkened windows shatter in a spray of glass and metal.

Looking up, Valiantine saw the top of the factory separate from the lower section and rise into the sky.

"Valiantine . . ." Cabot said, stumbling backward.

"Good *God*, Cabot!" the lieutenant shouted. "We were inside it! *We were inside the thing!*"

The giant wooden airship hung in the air over the crumbling building for only the span of a heartbeat or two. Turning in space, it floated over the edge of the factory's roof and toward the two agents.

Before he could yell to Cabot to run, it was upon them.

The great, wide hull dipped down and blanketed the space immediately above their heads, blocking out what little sun could be seen. In almost complete shadow now, Valiantine looked all around searching for sanctuary from the sure death that came at them from above.

Trees. His brain registered *trees*. His fingers brushed at Cabot's sleeve, but he did not solidly connect as he wished to. Something in his brain told him his partner was also moving, so he continued to run, imagining the airship to be inches from his head.

Diving underneath the clutch of scraggly trees, he got behind a tree trunk and dropped to his knees, praying it could withstand the weight of the onslaught. Cabot was suddenly next to him, slapping his arm, telling him he'd arrived, too.

Branches above their head cracked and snapped like gunshots. The entire tree shook and vibrated. The shadow of the airship retreated.

Then, gunshots exploded all around them.

Cabot returned fire at the shooter. A yell informed them the Treasury man's aim was good even under such arduous circumstances. Valiantine looked out past the tree and saw a wall in front of him; the side of the ship, no doubt, hovering only a few feet off the ground.

The lieutenant reached into his pocket and pulled out an object, the canister he procured from the attempt on the President's locomotive, still wrapped in his handkerchief but no longer smoking. In a flash, he twisted the metal pod, producing the smoke or vapor from it once more. The time had come for him to return the Trio's property.

"Get back," he ordered Cabot, and crawled out to the airship.

Valiantine's head swam. Whether it was the vox gas or the head trauma he'd received or a lifetime of hard knocks had finally resulted in the dementia suffered by old pugilists, he could not say, but he struggled through it toward the looming danger of the airship.

Just as he neared it, arriving mere feet from its hull, it lifted up into the sky. Valiantine stood up quickly, cocked his arm back and hurled the canister into space. He heard a clunk, and surmised that it landed somewhere on the ship itself.

Cabot caught him as he fell. Propping him back onto his feet, the two men watched as the great airship floated away, building up speed as it departed. It looked like a great wooden sailing vessel, yet swimming through the sky, not the ocean. The men cast their eyes over its rounded hull and the way the wood planking of its immense bulk fit together. It struck Valiantine that the ship should not be able to fly as it was, but it did, in complete disregard for any physical laws he knew.

The sound of a cannon firing made them swing their heads around to view the factory. The upper floors of it exploded and crumbled in on themselves.

"Covering their tracks?" Cabot asked.

"Perhaps," Valiantine responded, choking back a sob. "I do not know, Cabot."

A great flash of light filled the sky. The airship lurched. Fire belched from the upper portion of it, which to Valiantine's eye looked something like the deck of a sailing vessel. Thanks to the canister he'd thrown, the explosion meant for the President's train engulfed their enemies' unnatural transport.

Another fiery expulsion covered almost the entire airship in one blinding burst. Its prow dipped and the entire vehicle fell out of the sky, crashing to the ground with a sickening mélange of sound and fury.

In seconds, the wreckage was ablaze, strangely tinted tongues of fire engulfing it from end to end. Screams were carried across the field, giving the impression of a view into Hell itself.

"Come on," Cabot said, looking back and forth between his partner and the crash site.

Valiantine flowed into his wake, tremors wracking his body as the action subsided and he began to dwell upon what the future held.

Unable to approach the blazing enigma, government officials cordoned off the entire area from the local populace and began to wait it out. After almost twenty-four hours had passed since the crash, the fire had not died down in the slightest.

Upon returning to the District of Columbia from the outskirts of Philadelphia, Valiantine had sent a telegram to Eileen Warren, asking after her health and if he could possibly see her again.

Two days later, he and Cabot were ushered into the Oval Office at the Executive Mansion for a meeting with the President.

There they learned their Commander in Chief possessed what they believed to be a very good sense of the absurd when he announced he was creating an actual "Department A-13." Valiantine and Cabot would be its first two agents.

"You're Aero-Marshals now," the President said in all seriousness, "in actuality, not in pretense of a legitimate office of this government. We won't be issuing you new badges; the ones you already carry will suffice."

With the President's admonition that he had very real concerns over "incursions from other spheres" and the two men were now charged with "heading them off," they left the office and went out for a drink. It would take them a few more days, or even possibly a week, to digest it all.

They also noticed they'd been afforded no opportunity to decline the commissions.

Six days later, the wreckage still burned.

On the seventh day after the incident, Lieutenant Michael Valiantine sat quietly at a desk at the War Department in Washington, D.C. amidst a well-organized mix of papers, pens, and a few knick-knacks. To one side of the lieutenant sat a picture frame with a photo of a very handsome woman.

A nearby door opened and Cabot stepped through it, a bandage on his face and bruising still evident around both sets of knuckles. He approached his partner's desk and observed its tidy layout.

"What did she say?" Cabot asked, indicating the portrait of Eileen.

"Being the very intelligent woman that she is," Valiantine said without looking up, "she informed me that she would take the matter under very serious consideration."

After a moment of silence, the lieutenant glanced up at his partner. "So, what brings you here? We haven't been summoned at last, have we?"

Cabot nodded, running a finger along the brim of his new hat.

"Yes, in fact. The fire's gone out, Valiantine. We're needed."

After alighting from the coach, the Aero-Marshals approached the still-hot and steaming wreckage of what had become known in the intelligence community as "their" airship. It wasn't entirely accurate that the two agents were needed, but rather they were promised by the President himself they would be the first to view the debris once the fire had died down.

Handed long metal rods and cloaked in damp blankets and wearing extra-thick boots, Valiantine and Cabot waded into the wreckage, poking and prodding it as they went.

In less than a minute, they both tied handkerchiefs over their noses and mouths.

Here and there they could see human remains, but saw that identifying them would be quite a challenge. That said, they had no doubt the cabal of Gallows, Wellington, and Scarborough had met its end in the crash of the ship. It was very clear no one could have possibly escaped the fiery destruction.

What concerned them more was the absence of Awanai's body. After the agents saw they could not approach the wreckage after the crash, they had made their way over to the ruins of the factory. There, they had found no sign of the bandit's corpse, only a dried spot of blood where his head once rested on the cobblestones.

In the present, Valiantine and Cabot were hard-pressed to make much out in the debris of the airship. Mostly wood, apparently, its bones were picked rather clean by the strange fire.

A yell from behind brought them to another government man who was bent over a small pile of ash and charred wood. He had moved aside some of it to expose an object.

"What do ya make of it?" the man inquired of the Aero-Marshals, worrying his brow with one hand.

"A badge?" Valiantine pondered, prodding it with his metal rod.

"Another coin," Cabot suggested. The previous specimens had all but fallen apart a few days after the airship crash.

"Hmm, it's bigger than the others, then," the lieutenant said. "More like a plate of some sort."

Valiantine called for an insulated glove, the kind that might have been used in the foundry they witnessed in the building some days before. When it was brought to him, he donned it and reached down to pick up the round, metallic disc.

Turning it over in his gloved hand, he read its face. Cabot stared over his shoulder as he did so.

The raised words on the disc were very plain, and also very illuminating. They changed the two agents' lives completely, from that day forward and forever:

FIRST AIRSHIP OF THE EXECUTIVE DIRECTOR
OF THE INCORPORATED STATES OF AMERICA
1894

THE DEBRIEFING
Duane Spurlock

November 1897

M en had combed and sifted through the airship's wreckage for more than a week. The heat of the fires that followed the explosions had been so great that any metal found was twisted or melted beyond anyone's ability to identify its purpose. Only small bits of bone were recovered, so no one was even sure how many people had been aboard when the ship was engulfed.

The Aero-Marshals examined each piece of material recovered from the wreck. Neither Cabot nor Valiantine could add any useful information about the numbered and bagged bits brought from the crash site. They had no information to help identify the scraps brought out of the ash piles.

Cabot returned to the site twice in the hope of finding some clue. Valiantine would not join him for the trip. "There is a pall in the air there," the lieutenant explained. "It seems to choke me. I know we stopped the Trio from carrying out their plot. But even thinking about the ruins of that ship fills me with a sense of . . . of failure."

For the better part of a month, the Aero-Marshals wrote report after report based on their notes and memories. Cabot had an office in the Treasury Building, but he frequently could be found working in Valiantine's War Department office. A courier from the White House picked up files from their shared work space each week. The two men received no response from their reports. But putting their thoughts on paper—documenting their activities—served to empty them of much of the frustration and anxiety they had experienced, and so they stayed busy: comparing notes, asking questions of one another, and sharing meals at which they tried to make sense of the few things they had learned from Awanai, Wellington, Gallows, and Scarborough.

One morning the courier arrived, collected the new batch of files, and left behind an envelope marked with the seal of the President of the United States. Cabot opened it and read the missive it contained while Valiantine poured coffee for them both.

"The President thanks us for our very thorough reports," Cabot said. "He states the strains of our mission leading up to our encountering him on the train must have been considerable. He has been advised that we should share our information with an independent, neutral party."

"To what end?"

Cabot referred to the note. "Let's see, to help clarify our thoughts, promote genuine and rational deductions, and objectively judge our conclusions. Oh, and make sure we aren't yammering lunatics." Cabot looked up. "I added that last bit, but I think the President forgot to write that one down."

Valiantine lifted his cup. "What is the name of this paragon of lucidity?"

"Dr. Roderick Yarrow."

The lieutenant held his coffee without drinking. He frowned. "Yarrow?"

"You know him?"

Valiantine turned away and stared out the room's only window. "I know him. I saw him during my recuperative leave before we were assigned together. He's an alienist."

"Really?" Cabot scanned the letter again. "I've never met one. I thought they worked only with those unfortunates who already had been locked away in houses for the disturbed. I didn't realize they conferred with those for whom the jury was still out."

Valiantine smacked his desktop with his palm. His cup went clattering, spilling coffee onto the floor. "This is no joke, Cabot!" He held his breath a moment. When he resumed, he had regained control of his temper. "Yarrow offered me help. He has some standing among the President's advisors, clearly. Perhaps it won't be a bad idea. What we have seen and encountered . . . perhaps the doctor can help us make sure we are seeing what we should be seeing."

Cabot nodded. "And really seeing what we think we're looking at."

As directed by President McKinley's note, Cabot and Valiantine reached the door of Dr. Yarrow's home the next morning at ten o'clock. They were bundled against the late autumn chill, and the steam of their breathing hung in the air. The lieutenant turned the bell. A tall, slender servant opened the door. "Lieutenant Valiantine," he said. "How good to see you, sir."

"Brilson," Valiantine said. "Treasury Agent Cabot and I are to meet Dr. Yarrow."

"Absolutely, sir. This way."

Brilson took their hats and coats and showed them to a drawing room. It was a large, square room off the foyer, comfortably furnished with embroidered sofas and leather upholstered chairs. A Persian rug covered the floor. A second door with louvered panels was closed on the opposite side of the room. The servant said, "Dr. Yarrow will be with you presently." Then he exited to the foyer and closed the door behind him.

Other than the sofa and leather chairs, the room was furnished with a bookcase that covered one wall of the room and a single cabinet. Large hand-tinted engravings of flowering plants were framed and arranged on three walls of the room. Two walls offered two windows each; all but one was shuttered. Bars of morning light brightened the room. A small stove in a corner filled the space with warmth.

Dr. Yarrow entered through the door with louvered panels, which he closed behind him. "It is a pleasure to see you, Lieutenant Valiantine," he said as he advanced.

The lieutenant introduced Cabot. Handshakes all around. At Yarrow's gesture, the Aero-Marshals took seats on the embroidered sofa, and the doctor sat across from them in one of the leather chairs.

Yarrow was tall and, though he was tending toward stoutness, he looked like a man who had been devoted to vigorous activity rather than to bookish pursuits. He was in the neighborhood of fifty years old, but his hair was a rich black and rolled back from his forehead in thick waves, and he wore muttonchops that billowed out from his jowls. Seated in the black leather wingback chair, he resembled in some ways a bat, as though the chair's extensions were meant to funnel all sounds to his ears.

The doctor moved right to the point of their meeting: "Gentlemen, I have been given access to your voluminous reports on your very intriguing assignment. You have provided me some fascinating reading. Based on my examination of those documents, I should like to ask you some questions. You may answer with what you have discovered or deduced. Or my question may lead you to areas you have not yet considered. The ultimate goal of this exercise is to help you in understanding what you have faced in recent months."

"Understood," Valiantine said. Cabot nodded.

"Excellent. Let us begin." Yarrow steepled his fingers and touched them to his lips, then placed his hands in his lap. "What was the point of this conspiracy involving Major Wellington, Assistant Director Gallows, and Barnaby Scarborough?"

Valiantine said, "Their short-term goal appeared to be the assassination of President McKinley."

"And the long-term goal?"

"Based on things said by the Trio, as I call them, I believe they wanted to overthrow the existing government," the lieutenant said. "Or at least gain control of it through the agents they had in place through various agencies, in the way that Major Wellington and Gallows had taken over their roles."

"What do you mean, 'had taken over their roles'?"

Cabot spoke up: "Those men were imposters, sir. They more or less admitted that to us."

"More or less? And the men they replaced? Where are they?"

Cabot shook his head. "We don't know. We've found no clues even to when they may have been replaced. None of the men had any other family, and both lived alone."

"Hm." Yarrow briefly steepled his fingers again. "So, an effort to take control of the government. Not an invasion?"

"Not in the sense that we usually think of a military invasion," Valiantine said.

"And yet, your reports mention uniformed soldiers."

"Yes."

"Still," Yarrow said, "you report seeing fewer than one hundred at a time. This hardly sounds like an invasion."

"However," Cabot interjected, "besides the soldiers we actually saw, there were many men employed in the manufacturing floor of the outpost where we last encountered Awanai and the Trio. And a sailing ship or steamship comparable to the size of the airship that exploded would need a crew of at least one or two hundred men. Simply because we did not see large numbers doesn't mean they weren't present. And some may still be at large."

Yarrow appeared to consider. "What about this other group that seemed to be in conflict with this army led by the . . . ah, Trio? Are they still at large as well?"

Cabot nodded. "We can only assume so."

"Yet no sightings of either faction have been reported since the airship was destroyed?"

"No."

"Why are these two groups in conflict? Who do you think they represent? And do both have the ability to build these flying ships?"

Cabot glanced at Valiantine. The latter said, "We don't

know. We simply didn't witness enough or learn enough about the conflict to know much about the cause of their fight."

Cabot added, "We thought there were at least two ships. But we only ever saw one at a time. There have been no sightings reported since the wreck, so perhaps only one ever existed. And perhaps that other faction—the one challenging the Trio—was trying to capture the information for building a flying machine."

The doctor leaned forward. "Many 'perhaps.'"

Valiantine said, "As to the place these armies call home—again, we can only guess."

"The Trio spoke of *their world*," Cabot said. "I have seen utterly fantastic dime novels about travels to other planets, but I cannot accept that these men have come to our world from the moon or Mars. I can only surmise they are from another country or use 'our world' to mean another hemisphere."

"Indeed," the lieutenant added, "their uniforms looked somewhat Prussian."

Cabot said, "Perhaps 'our world' simply means there is some awkwardness in translating their language to English, and they aren't proficient with idioms. And it's quite possible the two groups come from the same country, but are opposing factions in some sort of civil war."

Yarrow tilted his head. "But the plate found in the wreckage of the ship said something about 'America,' did it not?"

Valiantine nodded. "Which is all the more confusing, but it at least suggests their home is in the New World, not Europe. Whatever their origin, it must be a country with advanced engineering capabilities. That would shorten the list."

Cabot said, "Unless Edgar Allan Poe and John Symmes were right, and a civilization has developed within the hollow Earth."

Dr. Yarrow stared at the Treasury agent. "Do you suppose that is possible, Mr. Cabot?"

Cabot's neck reddened. "No, I'm sorry. A moment of whimsy broke through my frustration at having witnessed so much but still knowing so little. I do apologize, it was completely inappropriate."

"Since you mention Mr. Poe, perhaps it is his Imp of the Perverse making itself known." Yarrow smiled.

Cabot attempted to smile in return. "Yes, you may be correct."

Valiantine cleared his throat. He caught Cabot watching him as he picked minute bits of lint from the sofa's embroidery. He moved his hands to his lap.

Dr. Yarrow spoke again. "It may be that we need some whimsy, gentlemen. In reading your reports, I've learned you were engaged in situations that exerted great stress upon your minds. You were in danger of losing your careers. You were, physically and mentally, in harm's way."

He gestured toward a wall. "Did you notice the botanical prints? A friend gave them to me years ago. But their purpose is not merely decorative. The bud opens up into the completely blooming flower. But the flower will not fully blossom until conditions are proper for it to do so."

Yarrow held up an index finger. "The mind is much like a flower. It is like a bud, closed about some mystery or problem, like the enigmas of this flying vessel you gentlemen are dealing with. You have worked hard, risked life and limb, and still have no satisfactory answers. The mind seeks order, and the order your minds seek regarding this airborne ship is closure. Only when these mysteries are resolved will you have closure, and then your minds will blossom again, free from worry."

The doctor smiled at his guests. "So, if levity will promote flowers over the mental weeds of confusion and frustration, then let us laugh." He chuckled in an artificial way that made the Aero-Marshals glance at one another.

"Dr. Yarrow," Cabot said, "since you are a neutral party reading our reports, what do you make of the situation as we have described it?"

Yarrow looked at his fingers before returning his gaze to his guests. "Like you, I am puzzled. By several things. For example, the likeness of the man named Carnavon to this strange person, Awanai."

"He was a mean, wicked creature." Valiantine's anger was obvious.

Cabot said, "The Trio suggested—obliquely—that they weren't simply imposters, but were related to the men they replaced in some way. Like . . . opposite sides of the same coin."

Yarrow's eyebrows rose. "Doppelgangers? Doubles?"

"Yes, that's it! Awanai was much more direct in stating Carnavon was his counterpart. Apparently Awanai developed the secret for the ship's ability to fly. He said Carnavon was on track to do the same. That's why Awanai murdered him."

"Ah. And did this have something to do with the coins?"

"No," Cabot said. "The coins simply seem to confuse everything further."

Yarrow leaned forward. This position, paired with the bat-eared shape of his chair, emphasized an appearance of the doctor looming over his guests. "How so?"

"Apparently the Trio's men aboard the airship used these coins while trading with at least three families in Kansas. Their minting remains a mystery—they are not U.S. coins, but perhaps they are badly designed counterfeits, for whatever reason." Cabot frowned. "Their design was bad enough that lawful authorities noticed them. I was initially brought into the airship mystery by investigating these coins."

"You were sent by the man posing as Gallows, correct?" Yarrow asked.

"Yes."

"But why?" Yarrow sat back. "If he was part of the conspiracy, why have it investigated?"

"Part of the Trio's camouflage."

"Ah. Please continue about the coins. They disappeared, I believe?"

"They seem to have been stolen."

"By whom?"

"Possibly they were recovered by the airship crew," Valiantine said.

"Possibly?"

"We think it's very likely they were removed by the faction opposing the airship army. Whoever stole them must have had mechanical techniques that allowed them to do so without leaving any sign of such."

Cabot added, "We think the opposing force used the stolen coins in Louisville."

"Allegedly finding them by the canal?" the doctor asked.

"Yes."

"To what purpose?"

Valiantine sighed. "Apparently to draw the airship faction into a trap. To perhaps gain the secrets to flying or to board the airship."

"Or," Cabot said, then he paused. "Or to capture a berserker."

Yarrow's fingers again formed a steeple. "You mean the monster?"

"It ties back to the coins," Cabot said. "We have surmised the cows—or perhaps there was only one cow, bartered multiple times—the cow was a sort of experiment. It produced milk that carried some quality or ingredient that caused the children to change into murderous beasts. After seeing the martial posturing of the airship agents, I can only surmise they were attempting to create some sort of berserker warrior—and exploited innocent children for this vile purpose."

"My goodness," Yarrow said. He dropped his hands to the arms of his chair.

"I think the one I shot in Louisville was Sam Brecker. He had tried to escape his captors. That's why we found victims there from both factions: he didn't want to return to the airship, and he didn't want to be captured by their enemies. He killed whoever tried to catch him. And the airship crew didn't want him found by anyone else."

"Hm." Yarrow stared at Cabot. "That all sounds . . . horrific."

Valiantine said, "We think Awanai was behind that mischief as well as making the ship fly."

"I see. And this flying—it was tied to the vapors?"

"Yes," the lieutenant said. "Apparently it was connected in some fashion to the meteorite Carnavon was working with."

"The vapor or gas had some deleterious effects, yes?"

"Certainly it affected our perceptions," Valiantine said. "And apparently those of the people on the ship."

Yarrow tapped the arms of the chair with his fingers. "You wrote that the principals—the Trio—seemed almost lethargic when they were aboard."

"Yes, and the soldiers did not respond in the sharp manner one would expect from military troops," the lieutenant said. "It probably helped save our lives and allow us to escape."

Cabot added, "It was like they were woozy . . . you might say they were drugged, as by doses of laudanum. Always they had someone playing music. This seemed so very odd, but we decided the music must have helped them keep their mental faculties engaged despite the effects of the vapor."

Yarrow nodded and rested his chin on the points of his fingers. "And the food the gentleman in Indiana mentioned—Perklee?"

"Just as excessive drink may lead to inebriated hedonism, apparently continual exposure to the vapor—the vox—can do something very similar."

"How strange." The doctor combed his fingers through his muttonchops. "Did the vapor contribute to the decomposition of the coins?"

Cabot had completely regained his composure and he spoke with confidence: "We thought that was a possibility."

"One of the Trio said all their metals suffered during the trip to our country—our 'world,' he called it," Valiantine said. "He may have meant the flying vapor corroded the coins and other metals during the trip. Again, it was another of their statements we've had to make guesses about."

Dr. Yarrow considered silently a few moments. He stood and walked to the unshuttered window. "Gentlemen, your descriptions of the singular events you have experienced match all that you have written in your reports, which I have perused with great interest." As the doctor spoke, he closed one of the window's shutters, so that light poured into the room only through half the window. He returned to his seat and asked, "What is your opinion about the threat to our nation? Is another flying ship at large?"

Valiantine answered: "We saw only one ship at a time—and not in such a way to identify any distinguishing characteristics to know whether we saw the same one each time or sighted more than one. Since there have been no sightings since the crash, it's likely only one ship ever was on the loose."

He raised a finger. "However, a second ship may be hiding out since the crash, or may have left the country to avoid stirring further uproar."

"Also," Cabot said, "we know the faction representing the airship had agents placed in roles of authority within the government. We know the Trio—barring other evidence yet to be found—are dead. But other agents, other doppelgangers may yet be in place, working unsuspected. So the threat remains."

Yarrow asked, "You were injured during your investigations, were you not? Both of you?"

Valiantine and Cabot nodded. The latter touched the fresh scar on his cheek.

"I would encourage you both to undergo medical examinations," the doctor said. "And consider your own exposure to the flying vapor. You describe in your reports the disorientation caused by the vox. We do not know the long-term effects of this material. The inappropriate responses of the Trio and the armed soldiers demonstrate the dangers to one's functions."

Yarrow gazed at the two several moments. "We have touched on the stresses your assignment created upon your physical and mental health. Coupled with the exposure to the vox, I wonder if some hallucinatory elements might have played upon your cognitive faculties and heightened the fantastic characteristics of your experiences."

Valiantine went completely still. Cabot sat bolt upright and narrowed his eyes. "Are you calling into question the veracity of our reports?"

Yarrow raised a placating hand. "On the contrary, I believe you have documented very accurately what you perceived during the events. But it is widely understood that perception sometimes paints reality with a brush colored by an emotion- or perception-altering palette. The vox, for example."

"The wreckage of the airship is an undeniable reality," Valiantine said in a quiet voice.

"True," Yarrow said, "but we have only your description of its character before the crash to rely upon."

Silence from the visitors.

Dr. Yarrow resumed: "I am not attempting to undermine your work. You have been through a difficult period. I am here to help you and to support the President's efforts to secure our country against foreign incursions." He looked each man in the eyes several seconds. "I have two recommendations for you. First, I ask you to comb and sift through your recollections and impressions of the events you experienced. Measure them against what is reasonable and against the hard evidence that remains from your investigations."

The Aero-Marshals did not reply.

Yarrow continued: "Second, I urge you to rest from your labors. You have worked diligently, under great stress, in service to your President and your country. You have continued to focus your mental energies on deducing solutions to the mysteries raised by the flying machine. But it is time for you to rest. Relax. No flying ship sightings have been reported since the wreck. No reports of strange military forces have been received. Really, how many agents could possibly remain in place? How many doppel-gangers could realistically exist? Now that the authorities know how their agencies have been infiltrated, any false agents will eventually be discovered."

The doctor stood. "You were given a mission—whatever ruse may have lain behind it—and you more than succeeded in carrying it out. Despite the will and coercion of your false superiors, you succeeded in revealing the black plot against the nation and the President. Gentlemen, celebrate your success. Close the file on this mission. Move on to more pleasant concerns."

Yarrow smiled and spread his hands. "I am sorry, gentlemen, but I have another appointment to get to. I so appreciate your coming here. Please feel welcome to visit again." The Aero-Marshals stood, and Yarrow shook their hands. "Thank you for your service to your country. You are fine examples for your peers." He opened the door to the foyer. "Good day, gentlemen. Brilson will see you out."

Minutes later, standing by the street, Cabot shivered and pulled his coat closer. "So, do you suppose we were judged sane or dangerously mad?" he asked.

Valiantine adjusted his hat. "We knew we would encounter resistance when we began to discuss these matters in detail outside our own company." They started walking to the corner. "And Dr. Yarrow must keep the wellbeing of the country in mind. He is a doctor. Our veracity, our health are all part of his concern."

"Hm." Cabot glanced back at the doctor's residence. "He is correct about one thing. We must remain vigilant."

"He is correct in another, as well," Valiantine said. "We are weary. Both in mind and body. We need to accept that we have resolved the immediate threats. It is time to focus on the future." The lieutenant took a deep breath and held it a few moments before releasing it in a gust. "I, for one, am ready."

Dr. Yarrow watched Valiantine and Cabot through his half-shuttered window. Behind him, the louver-paneled door opened. A wheelchair came into the room, pushed by Brilson. Seated in the chair, wearing an embroidered robe and a lap blanket, was the man who called himself Awanai. A large pad covered his left eye. It was held in place by a bandage wrapped around his head.

"You heard?" Yarrow asked.

"Oh yes," Awanai said. "Quite well."

Yarrow glanced once more out the window before closing the remaining shutter. He turned to face the man in the wheelchair. "They are filled with suppositions, doubts, confusion, indignation. But," and he paused to touch his fingertips together before his chest, as if in prayer, "they *do* know more than they realize."

Awanai stared at the doctor several moments. Then he touched his forefinger to his cheek below his remaining eye. "Then they will bear watching."

ABOUT THE AUTHORS

Jim Beard hunts the biggest of all game: good storytelling. With years of comic book collecting and obsessive amounts of science fiction, fantasy, and pulp reading under his belt, he frequently startles his Northwest Ohio neighbors with his constant muttering and note-making. Beyond that, Jim's works include *Sgt. Janus Spirit-Breaker*, *Monster Earth*, *Monster Aces*, the Captain Action pulp novels, and *Gotham City 14 Miles*, a comprehensive look at the 1966 Batman TV series.

Duane Spurlock comes from a long line of long-winded story-tellers and near-sighted doodlers. He writes in a number of genres and occasionally illustrates books, including Brian J. Showers' *The Bleeding Horse and Other Ghost Stories*, which won the 2008 Children of the Night Award from The Dracula Society. He lives with his family in Kentucky, where they garden, whistle, read folktales, and tell one another stories when not climbing bean stalks and hunting trolls.

Meteor House Titles

THE WORLDS OF PHILIP JOSÉ FARMER
Anthology Series edited by Michael Croteau

Volume 1: Protean Dimensions
Volume 2: Of Dust and Soul
Volume 3: Portraits of a Trickster
Volume 4: Voyages to Strange Days

WOLD NEWTON SERIES

Doc Savage: His Apocalyptic Life by Philip José Farmer

The Khokarsa Series
Exiles of Kho by Christopher Paul Carey
Flight to Opar (Restored Edition) by Philip José Farmer
Hadon, King of Opar by Christopher Paul Carey

The Pat Wildman Series
The Evil in Pemberley House by Philip José Farmer and Win Scott Eckert
The Scarlet Jaguar by Win Scott Eckert

The Phileas Fogg Series
Phileas Fogg and the War of Shadows by Josh Reynolds

SCIENCE FICTION ADVENTURE

The Abnormalities of Stringent Strange by Rhys Hughes
Airship Hunters by Jim Beard and Duane Spurlock

www.meteorhousepress.com

www.ingramcontent.com/pod-product-compliance
Lightning Source LLC
Chambersburg PA
CBHW030332030726
47499CB00003B/740